# "Rave On"

## Classic Texas Music Quotes

# Classic Texas Quotes

**Kirk Dooley, Series Editor**
**Kent Gamble, Series Illustrator**

"...'Til the Fat Lady Sings"
Classic Texas Sports Quotes
**Alan Burton**

"Read My Lips"
Classic Texas Political Quotes
**Kirk Dooley and Eben Price**

"Rave On"
Classic Texas Music Quotes
**Alan Burton**

# "Rave On"

## Classic Texas Music Quotes

Alan Burton

Illustrations by Kent Gamble

Texas Tech University Press

For Mae and Bob

This book was set in New Century Schoolbook and Tekton and printed on acid-free paper that meets the guidelines for permanence and durability of the Committee on Production Guidelines for Book Longevity of the Council on Library Resources.  ∞

Art by Kent Gamble
Cover design by Lisa Camp

Manufactured in the United States of America.

**Library of Congress Cataloging-in-Publication Data**
Rave on : classic Texas music quotes / Alan Burton [editor] ;
    illustrations by Kent Gamble.
        p.    cm.
    Includes bibliographical references and index.
    ISBN 0-89672-370-4 (pbk. : alk. paper)
    1. Musicians—Texas—Quotations.  2. Music—Texas—Miscellanea.
  I. Burton, Alan, 1956-
ML65.R39   1996
780'.9764—dc20                                              96-18220
                                                                CIP


96 97 98 99 00 01 02 03 04/ 9 8 7 6 5 4 3 2 1

Texas Tech University Press
Box 41037
Lubbock, TX  79409-1037  USA
1-800-832-4042

iv

# CONTENTS

v

# Foreword

Some of you may have noticed that Texas has spawned a disproportionately large share of famous musicians. This has been going on for quite a while now—long enough, in fact, that it might be justly dubbed a bona fide phenomenon. Outlanders tend to explain away this particular circumstance by pointing to the sheer size of the state. "Of course you have a lot of musical stars," they say. "Yours is the second largest state in the Union." At that point, I usually ask them to list for me all the famous Alaskan musicians, and that usually shuts them up (except, of course, for the ones who start harping about California, and then I have to explain to them patiently that practically none of those big-time music stars out in the Golden State are actually from there. In fact, a helluva lot of them are from here.). So, when it comes to renowned Texas musicians, the fact remains that their numbers are unusually great and they span many generations. It should also be noted (no pun intended) that the musicians and the music of Texas are as diverse as Texas culture itself, as unpredictable and varied as the Texas weather and terrain. Every corner of the state has produced musicians of acclaim—from the piney thickets of

East Texas to the Rio Grande; from the arid Panhandle to the rolling Hill Country to the Gulf coast—and their music, their words and attitudes are affected not only by the rich cultural stew that is Texas but by the very land and sky; the long, straight highways; the endless horizon; the motels and small-town honky-tonks; the big cities with their glitzy clubs and gleaming skyscrapers. These things and much more are a part of the collective consciousness of musicians from the Lone Star State.

Texas musicians may have one thing (if any) in common with Texas politicians. That is to say they are, by and large, a colorful, often eccentric bunch who are given to uttering provocative and controversial remarks—sometimes only when pressed, other times quite voluntarily. These remarks, in most cases, are the well-seasoned by-product of the wide and often unusual array of experiences that characterize the typical Texas musician. The Lone Star State is a paradoxical place, blown by the winds of contrariness. Its musical sons and daughters are a manifestation of the dichotomy that is inherent in the culture: liberal-conservative, religious-secular, patriotic-rebellious, conformist-maverick. At the top of the list—the thread that runs through the soul of all Texas musicians—is the conflict between going and staying; the burning desire, born of loneliness and perceived dissimilarity, to escape or transcend the culture coupled with a deep longing to be a part of it. The struggle to balance and make sense of this ethos is

embedded in all of us—singers, songwriters, players. That's the highfalutin analysis of our kind. Others would simply say that we do what we do to get money and attention from the opposite sex (not necessarily in that order). In any case, when one has had enough Lone Star beer bottles hurled in the direction of one's head, been taken to the women's jail by an arresting officer because of the length of one's hair (remember the 60s?), traveled the globe, dined with the powerful and the common folk; when one has been equally honored and reviled on home turf, a certain insight—a very ironic way of looking at the world—emerges. This book captures that twisted, humorous vision quite well. Enjoy.

Don Henley

# Preface

## I.

In words, "Rave On" is both a celebration of Texas music and a tribute to its musicians.

In a state that is known for being "bigger and better," music is certainly no exception.

Just about every popular form of music known to man has roots in the Lone Star State. Even more impressive is the sheer number of talented musicians who have called Texas home.

From the cowboy crooning of Gene Autry to the high-tech blues/rock of ZZ Top, Texas boasts a virtual Who's Who of musical heritage. Some of the more familiar names include Willie Nelson, Roy Orbison, Buddy Holly, Bob Wills, George Jones, Janis Joplin, and Kenny Rogers—all Texas natives. And don't forget Meat Loaf, Vanilla Ice, and Van Cliburn (a rocker, a rapper, and a world-class pianist).

"Rave On" is a collection of meaningful, memorable, and in some cases humorous quotes, by and about some of these great musicians and their profession. These

ix

talented people have entertained us with their music and lyrics; now they enlighten us through another medium—the spoken word.

## II.

The song "Rave On" was a minor/major success for Lubbock's Buddy Holly and the Crickets. Released in 1958, "Rave On" only reached number 39 on Billboard's Top 100 singles list in the United States. However, in Britain the song made the top five on the national charts.

According to John Goldrosen's book, *The Buddy Holly Story*, "Rave On" was an important piece of work:

"To many people, 'Rave On' is the most exciting recording the Crickets ever made: the title has become a byword for Holly's frenetic style. . . . A joyful and driving performance, 'Rave On' epitomizes the good feeling of rock 'n' roll. The song offers the most perfect introduction to Holly's vocal gimmickry—for who else but Buddy Holly could make a rising six-syllable word out of 'well,' as he does at the very opening of the song?"

—Alan Burton

# "Rave On"
## Classic Texas Music Quotes

1

2

ROCK 'N' ROLL
AND ALL THAT JAZZ

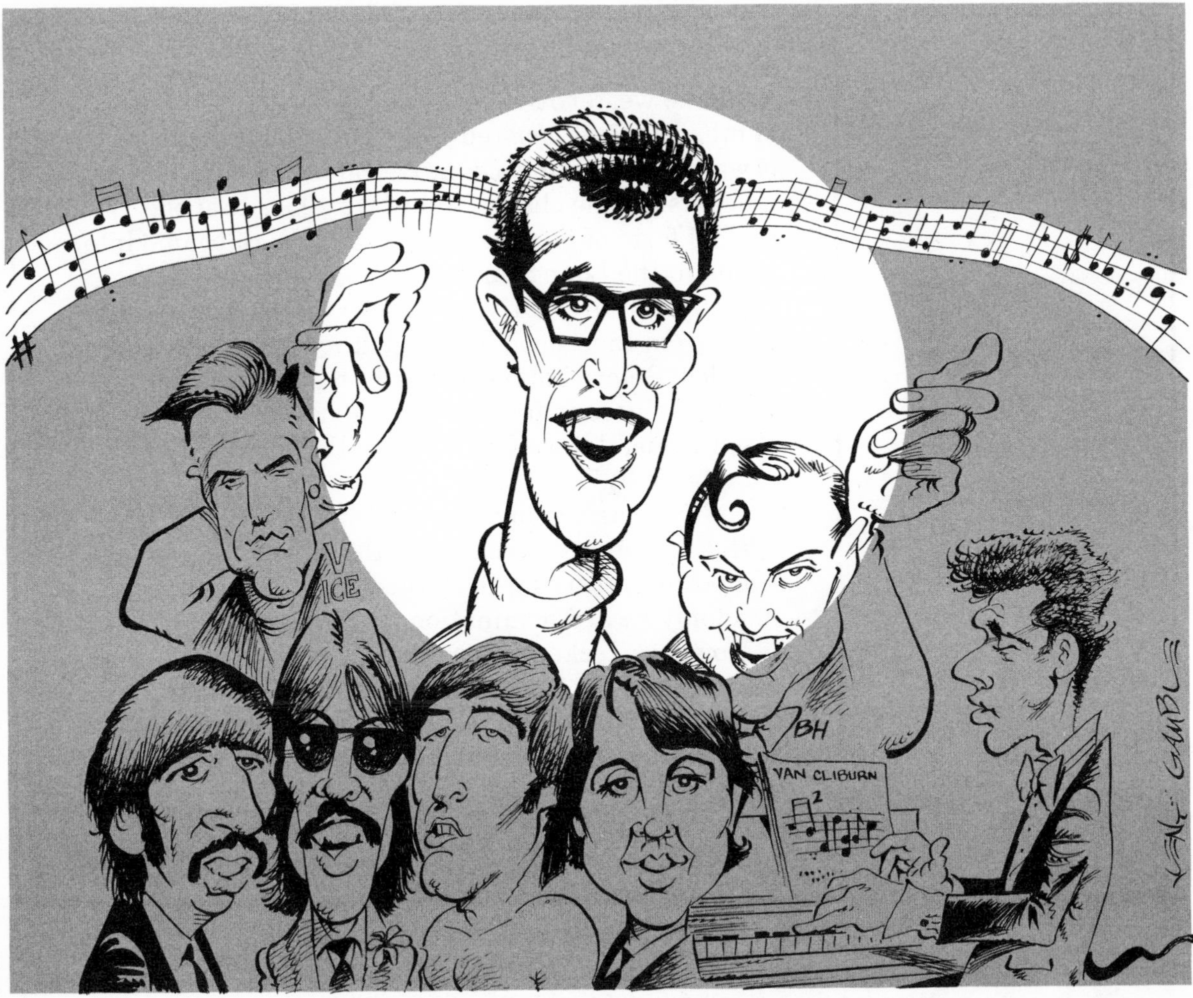
V
ICE
BH
VAN CLIBURN

4

Blues, western swing, and country are three types of music long associated with the state of Texas. But it wasn't until Lubbock native Buddy Holly and the Crickets hit the charts in the late 1950s that the radical form of music known as rock 'n' roll came into vogue in the Lone Star State.

Holly's style greatly influenced the sounds of that band from Liverpool, England, known as the Beatles. Before his tragic death in a 1959 plane crash, Holly contributed such memorable songs as "Peggy Sue," "Rave On," "That'll Be The Day," and "Maybe Baby."

Holly's music enjoyed renewed popularity in 1978 with the Hollywood release of the movie, *The Buddy Holly Story,* starring Gary Busey (who earned an Academy Award nomination for best actor).

However, rock 'n' roll wasn't always the most popular form of expression among small town residents. Thirty-five years ago, the "evils of rock 'n' roll" was a popular theme preached from numerous Texas pulpits.

Nevertheless, Holly professed his preference for rock: "We like this kind of music [rock]. Jazz is strictly for the stay-at-homes."

"I am not really into rock and roll. Rock may be good to dance to for kids, but you can dance to country music, too."

Country musician Tanya Tucker
*The New Country Music Encyclopedia*

 ☆ ☆ ☆

"The story has got pretty crowded as to who was the Father of Rock and Roll. I haven't done much in life except that. And I'd like to get credit for it."

Bill Haley, leader of Bill Haley and the Comets
*Rock Lives*

☆ ☆ ☆

"Rock and Roll?  Why, man, that's the same kind of music we've been playing since 1928! . . . It's just basic rhythm and has gone by a lot of different names in my time. It's the same, whether you follow just a drum beat like in Africa or surround it with a lot of instruments. The rhythm's what's important."

Bob Wills, leader of the Texas swing band, Bob Wills and the Texas Playboys
*San Antonio Rose: The Life and Music of Bob Wills*

5

6

"Rock 'n' roll actually wasn't invented by anybody, and it's not just black and white either. It's Mexican and Appalachian and Gaelic and everything that's come floating down the river."

Singer/songwriter T-Bone Burnett
*The Great Rock 'n' Roll Quote Book*

 ☆ ☆ ☆

"Buddy Holly was the gentleman of rockabilly, the first soft rocker."

Writer Nick Tosches
*Small Talk, Big Names—40 Years of Rock Quotes*

☆ ☆ ☆

"If anybody asks you what kind of music you play, tell him 'pop.' Don't tell him 'rock 'n' roll' or they won't even let you in the hotel."

Rock 'n' roll musician Buddy Holly
*The Great Rock 'n' Roll Quote Book*

"It was teenage music, simple, appealing, something the guitar player could play and sing and hum along, with nothing far out, no hard chords, no hard lyrics, simple—'I love you, Peggy Sue, with a love so rare and true'—played with a great feel. They played that singable, pretty, listenable music with such a great feel that it was just magic."

Musician Sonny Curtis (a member of Holly's band the Crickets), on the appeal of Buddy Holly's music
*Prairie Nights to Neon Lights: The Story of Country Music in West Texas*

"What rock and roll was then is what country is today. Waylon Jennings had a really great rock and roll band but with a steel guitar so he could call it country."

Sonny Curtis, on rock and roll in the late 1950s
*Prairie Nights to Neon Lights: The Story of Country Music in West Texas*

"It's just entertainment, and the kids who like to identify their youthful high spirits with a solid beat are thus possibly avoiding other pursuits that could be more harmful to them."

Bill Haley, on rock music
*The New Book of Rock Lists*

7

"The Duran Duran songs were demonic and Tina Turner and Mick Jagger did their bumping, grinding duet . . . face-to-face, belly-to-belly . . . It's hard to look at something like that and think, 'I'm going to send money to starving kids.'"

Pop/gospel musician Pat Boone, on the Live Aid concert
*Rock Talk*

"Rock 'n' roll's gone so rank now. Some guy gets out there with a feather in his cap and a jockey strap on and paints hisself all up and screams and the audience is goin' crazy 'cause they're all on dope but that's not music."

Buddy Holly's brother, Larry Holley
*Buddy Holly, A Biography*

"Rock hasn't had any honesty in so long it's pitiful. The last real honesty that rock and roll music ever had was Fats Domino and Chuck Berry and part of the Beatles."

Country musician Waylon Jennings
*The Outlaws: Revolution in Country Music*

"The whole scene was the most decadent thing I've ever witnessed—like a scene from Dante's Inferno. I saw pretty young girls coming up the steps of the arena on their hands and knees, overcome by noise, drink, pot—I don't know what—crawling to get relief."

Pat Boone on attending an Ozzy Osbourne heavy metal concert
*Sherman Democrat*

"The glitter rock, the codpiece rock, the naked-man rock can only last so long. Music keeps on changing; it's ready for another change right now. But people will pay to see the damnedest things. Like I think paying to see David Bowie is a very weird thing to do. But I imagine there must be a place for what he does; he's a success."

Country singer/songwriter Steve Fromholz, 1974
*The Improbable Rise of Redneck Rock*

"People are tired of this cosmic cowboy shit. They're ready to rock and roll."

Country/rock musician Doug Sahm of the Texas Tornadoes, 1974
*The Improbable Rise of Redneck Rock*

10

"People don't want good music anymore. They want stages blowing up and shit. The blues has always been neglected. Most of the good bluesmen had to quit or change their music when the Beatles and the Rolling Stones came along."

Austin blues club owner Clifford Antone
*Stevie Ray: Soul to Soul*

"In the 1960s, when white kids first started hearing blues, they didn't really know what it was. It sounded like rock 'n' roll but it wasn't. It took them awhile to figure out that blues is the root."

Blues guitarist Albert Collins
*Meeting the Blues: The Rise of the Texas Sound*

"It's hard for me to say where blues stops and rock 'n' roll starts. I've always played both of them, and to me, they're the same thing."

Blues guitarist Johnny Winter
*Meeting the Blues: The Rise of the Texas Sound*

"The blues tell a true story. They sing about the real mean and rotten things that can happen to you."

Blues guitarist Albert King
*Janis Joplin: Piece of my Heart*

"The blues is something that happens in everyday life. To my idea, the blues is something simple. It doesn't have to be about a lady. Sometimes your boss man makes you mad and you have to feel it on the inside, but you can't quit it because otherwise you wouldn't have one. When your lady makes you mad and you know you can't live without her, that's the blues."

Blues guitarist Little Joe Blue
*Meeting the Blues: The Rise of the Texas Sound*

"Blues is to soothe. It makes people who were feelin' bad feel good again. That's the true feeling of the blues. It's not a depressing music, as some folks have been led to believe."

Blues guitarist Stevie Ray Vaughan
*Stevie Ray: Soul to Soul*

12

"Texas is where I grew up, where I learned to play white country music, French music, and blues. The blues depends on what you're feeling, but it's also supposed to be an explanation."

Blues musician Clarence "Gatemouth" Brown
*Meeting the Blues: The Rise of the Texas Sound*

"To me, blues is getting your feelings out. It's not a particularly fast thing, a lot of people think it's crying in your beer, let's all feel bad together, but it's really not that way at all. The blues has a lot of up songs, your experiences. Even if you're talking about the bad, you can feel better because you can relate to it. If it's done right, it should make you feel like you're sharing the experience."

Johnny Winter
*Meeting the Blues: The Rise of the Texas Sound*

"The blues will always be around. It will never die. It's something that will always be here. Blues is the basic foundation of the music."

Blues guitarist Pee Wee Crayton
*Meeting the Blues: The Rise of the Texas Sound*

"There is more of an acceptance of blues today. It probably has a lot to do with Stevie Ray Vaughan. The music is real, there's no pretensions. You just come and get it."

Dallas blues guitarist Hash Brown, 1995
*The Dallas Morning News*

 ☆ ☆ ☆

"The only thing that divides the blues from the gospel are the words. Where you say 'Lord' in gospel, in blues you say 'daddy.'"

Gospel musician Beulah "Sippie" Wallace
*Meeting the Blues: The Rise of the Texas Sound*

 ☆ ☆ ☆

"Blues and country are the same thing, just the moods are different. It all comes from life experiences."

Houston record producer Huey P. Meaux
*Rolling Stone*

13

**14**

"I think black music and country music are a beat apart: One man singing about a woman he can't keep and the other about a woman he can't get."

Waylon Jennings
*Country Musicians*

"I sing white man's blues."

Country musician George Jones
*The New Country Music Encyclopedia*

"Country music and blues music are basically about the same thing. It's men singing about working and the women they love. That's country music."

Waylon Jennings
*The Dallas Morning News*

☆ ☆ ☆

"In their true forms, country and blues are incredibly close first cousins, and I could never draw a line between them. Coming up musically in Austin, I didn't worry about drawing that line."

Country musician Lee Roy Parnell
*Country America*

"If it sounds country, then it is."

Musician/actor Kris Kristofferson
*Texas Rhythm, Texas Rhyme*

"Bob Wills began to bridge the gap between country
and western music and big band swing during the
forties by presenting the simpler C&W songs in
more sophisticated updated arrangements, a
compromise that resulted in thousands of dedicated
West Coast fans, attracted by the sight of cowboy
attired musicians who sounded more like
city-slickers."

Music writer/commentator George T. Simon
*San Antonio Rose: The Life and Music of Bob Wills*

"Western swing was just about the only kind of
country music you could hear in the state of Texas
until Hank Williams came along. Western swing
was jazz, any way you want to look at it."

Country musician Willie Nelson
*Willie: An Autobiography*

15

16

"Clay leans a little more toward the blues kind of pop kind of thing, I think. Mark I think leans more toward the George Jones kind of thing in a lot of ways. Mine I think is more down the alley where I wanted it to be, more of the Strait kind of thing and then a little bit of Western Swing thrown in there and twisted in there."

Country musician Tracy Byrd, comparing his music to Clay Walker's, Mark Chesnutt's, and George Strait's
*Sherman Democrat*

"It's popular because, first of all, it's a damn good tune. To me, it's a regional love affair with both the instrument that plays it—the fiddle—and the ease with which it is played and danced. And it's a great socializing tool."

Ethnic music expert Jim Fox, on the "Cotton-Eyed Joe"
*The Dallas Morning News*

"If I do a country song, I pretty much go for what will sound country on it.  Now, I put a lot of rock into things, but I wouldn't call it country-rock.  There's a fine line in there where you are ruining a country song or you are adding to it."

Country musician Junior Brown
*The Dallas Morning News*

"Texas people really love their music. You get honky tonk, swing, Cajun, and blues all rolled up because the people live to dance."

Country musician Mark Chesnutt
*Country America*

"It's really weird. I've never had a hit record. I wrote this song that somebody else cut that was never a single and never got a lot of airplay. And it became this catalyst, the definitive progressive country thing. It's always been this bastard child."

Country singer/songwriter Ray Wylie Hubbard, on "Redneck Mother,"
1993
*D Magazine*

17

18

"I'm a real romantic about country music. For me, country music is at its best coming out of the dashboard of a '49 Ford."

Country singer/songwriter Rodney Crowell
*The New Country Music Encyclopedia*

☆ ☆ ☆

"You know what you get when you play country music backwards? You get your wife back, your house back, and your car back."

Country musician Clint Black
*Talkin' Country: Down-Home Philosophy and Advice from Country's Biggest Stars*

☆ ☆ ☆

"To me, country music is an art form, always changing. Even classical music doesn't sound the same from one decade to another. The instruments and the arrangements have evolved from one century to the next."

Barbara Mandrell
*Get to the Heart: My Story*

"Historically, I guess it's true that American country music has its roots in the people who came over from England, Ireland, Scotland, and Wales and settled in the Appalachian Mountains then moved out west. But I say that country music is pure American, and it continues to evolve."

Country musician Barbara Mandrell
*Get to the Heart: My Story*

"If we're going to have country music, we need to save some country."

Don Henley, amplifying his views on the need to protect the environment
*Common Thread* (notes from CD booklet)

19

**20**

"A lot of people tell me they don't like country music, but they like what I'm doing . . . . What I did was incorporate some of the other ideas I'd had in music to make it more appealing without ruining the country aspects. It's a balance, a tightrope that you walk; you don't want to throw in something that doesn't fit. I just blended in blues licks and Hawaiian and bluegrass and rock and . . ."

Junior Brown, 1995
*The Met*

"The mentality of country music has become a lot like that of rock—you grind out as many new artists as you can."

Country musician Charley Pride
*Pride: The Charley Pride Story*

"Actually, I blame Alabama for the demise of country. They crossed over, everyone followed them, and no one came back."

Country musician/author Kinky Friedman, attributing the cross-over trend to the band Alabama
*Texas Monthly, 1993*

"These days in country music, if you're over 25 and don't wear a hat, forget it."

Country musician Larry Gatlin, on radio's "new country format," 1995
*Parade Magazine*

"Country music is becoming like the PGA. You have the regular tour and the seniors' tour. Branson is the seniors tour."

John Dainer, Charley Pride's road manager, on the phenomenon in Branson, Missouri
*Pride: The Charley Pride Story*

"Well, I'm really not much of a guitar player. I found that out when I was doing all those folk gigs. I figured that country was the easiest way to get where I wanted to be. What I do is not really country, but it's got a lot of country flavor. I appreciate straight country, but I just don't like to play it all that much."

Country musician Rusty Wier, 1974
*The Improbable Rise of Redneck Rock*

21

22

"Folksingers have always been treated like the 'F' word."

Austin singer/songwriter Nanci Griffith, 1995
*The Dallas Morning News High Profile*

"Anybody can be a pop singer, but to be a country singer is tough."

Kris Kristofferson
*Written in my Soul: Rock's Great Songwriters Talk about Creating their Music*

☆ ☆ ☆

"Contemporary music can appear easy to sing, but really it's the toughest kind of vocalizing you can do."

Pop/gospel musician B. J. Thomas
*Home Where I Belong*

☆ ☆ ☆

"It's harder writing rap music than it is writing singing music. You gotta think up more words. You have to have a story line behind it."

White rapper Vanilla Ice (a.k.a. Robby Van Winkle)
*Rolling Stone*

"Personally, I like it. Disco is bright, major key music. I like to try and write good lyrics to it. Also, it's a natural outgrowth of Motown and Philly music, which means a lot to me. Disco showed me how to move from rock and blues, but still keep the energy and freedom that rock gives you."

Musician Boz Scaggs, on disco music, 1978
*Circus Magazine*

"Texas and Chicago were linked by a train line, so the music from those two places is a lot closer than you think."

Stevie Ray Vaughan
*Stevie Ray: Soul to Soul*

"There was a lot of musical cross-pollination that went on in Texas that didn't take place elsewhere . . . . You have a tremendous melting pot there. Everything from the strong German tradition, the polka bands, Western swing, Mexican music . . . . The races didn't seem to be as rigidly segregated as they were in the lower South."

Writer/musicologist/producer Pete Welding
*The Dallas Morning News*

23

24

"Being from Texas there's so much to be proud of. You have to be good because look at who you're following. All of the great bands—western swing, jazz, blues, Mexican music—there's so much to live up to, and I think that's why the musicianship in Texas is what it has been."

Blues musician Angela Strehli
*Meeting the Blues: The Rise of the Texas Sound*

☆ ☆ ☆

"It's garage band music. Five- or six-chord, self-taught folk. I listen to all kinds of music and I filter it all down to this little twelve-bar blues, Texas thing that I grew up with and learned as a child. And I instill a feeling of hope and optimism in the face of a lot of bullshit."

Rock/pop musician Steve Miller, describing his style of music, 1993
*Rolling Stone*

"But classical music is not entertainment, and I feel viciously strong about that. Classical music is forever. It is not entertainment. Entertainment is something that is here today and may be gone tomorrow."

Classical pianist Van Cliburn
*Van Cliburn*

"East Texas has always been a singing area. Our pioneers came from the Deep South singing their familiar religious and work songs. Later, when modern country music came along, Jim Reeves and Tex Ritter brought fame to this region."

Historian/teacher Leila Belle LaGrone
*Texas Highways*

"He's got me listening to—what's it called?—Nine Inch Nails? Sounds like a train wreck sometimes, but every once in awhile you hear something good."

Waylon Jennings, on his teenage son's musical tastes
*You're the Reason our Kids are Ugly and Other Gems of Country Music Wisdom*

25

# 26

**BEER, HIPPIES, MUD,
AND NAKED WOMEN**

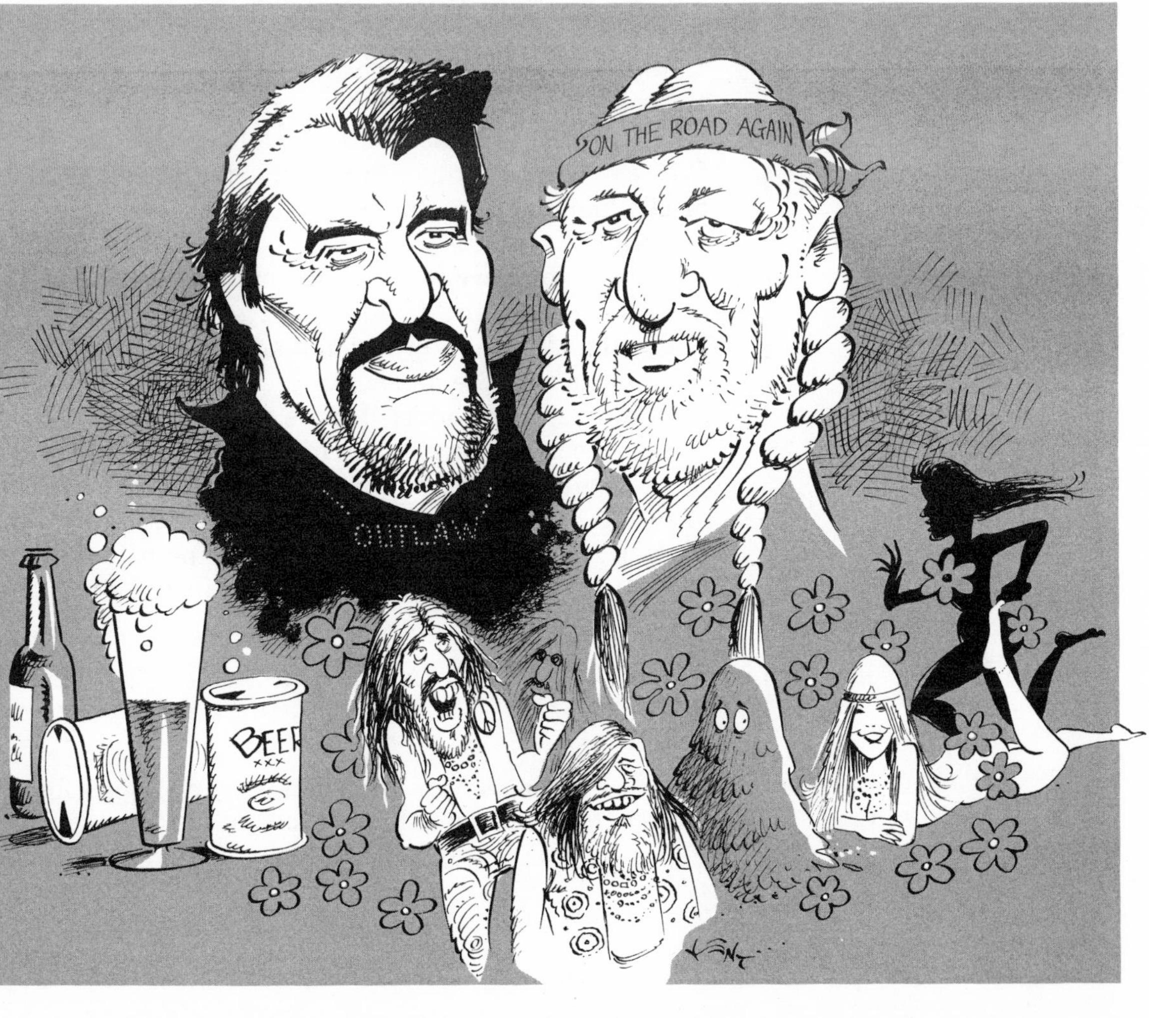
ON THE ROAD AGAIN
OUTLAW
BEER
XXX

28

Roy Orbison studied to be a geologist at North Texas State University. Steve Miller was planning to be a literature professor. Buddy Holly considered a future in engineering or drafting. John Denver briefly majored in architecture at Texas Tech University.

Luckily, these were vocational whims. Each of these Texas-bred musicians would go on to win national and even international acclaim for their contributions to the music world.

Of course, there are still those who don't get it. Those who ask: "Why choose music as a career?"

Texas musician Ray Wylie Hubbard has an answer. "You're twenty-six years old, and you're playing Willie's picnics. There's beer, hippies, mud, naked women. Why would you want to do anything else?"

"I couldn't think of anything better than singing for money and having pretty girls look at me."

Country musician Johnny Lee, on beginning his musical career as a youth
*Lookin' for Love*

"Look, we're all maladjusted little weirdos or we wouldn't be doing this."

Eagles member Don Henley
*Rock Talk*

"Once in a lifetime, a Brenda Lee comes along—someone who came out of the womb singing, someone with God-given talent like Dolly or Tanya. LeAnn fills that bill.  She's an extraordinarily talented young woman and hers is not a kiddie act; hers is a voice that needs to be heard."

Country music writer Robert K. Oermann on 13-year-old country singer LeAnn Rimes, 1996
*Country Weekly*

☆ ☆ ☆

"It used to be one of my goals to become one of the youngest recording artists in country music with a number one hit. Tanya Tucker beat me by about ten years."

Country musician Clay Walker, 1996
*The Dallas Morning News*

29

30

"Ice is like a new New Kid on the Block . . . . I see his rap career as short-lived—my goal is to have a couple of successful albums, then have him go into movies."

Tommy Quon, manager for rapper Vanilla Ice, 1991
*Rolling Stone*

 ☆ ☆ ☆

"I can certainly see Willie becoming as big a movie actor as Barbra Streisand."

Movie producer/director Sydney Pollack on Willie Nelson
*Willie: An Autobiography*

 ☆ ☆ ☆

"He's an outstanding singer, but he should stick with singing. I've heard Troy Aikman sing, and I don't think he can be in Mac Davis's league. But by the same token, Mac better stay away from football."

Former Dallas Cowboy coach Jimmy Johnson, on Mac Davis's performance in the movie *North Dallas Forty*
*The Dallas Morning News*

"I would only do a very serious film . . . . Playing music is one emotion that no matter how talented an actor or an actress is, cannot be emulated successfully. Whenever an actor tries to play a pianist or violinist, he doesn't look right in the musical scenes."

Classical pianist Van Cliburn
*Van Cliburn*

"It's what I always wanted to do. I went to college for four years and studied, but I never had any intention of doing anything except this."

Don Henley, on rock 'n' roll, 1990
*Rolling Stone*

"My goal in life was to be a successful recording artist and to travel around the world and sing in places I had never been."

Johnny Lee
*Lookin' for Love*

32

"I figured out what I wanted to do with my life at an early age. Then I set about doing it, which was playing guitar. I didn't have much choice, really—it wasn't like I was gonna go to college."

Blues-rock guitarist Charlie Sexton, 1995
*The Dallas Morning News*

"Rock and roll was always about being an alternative, an opportunity for poor kids who were going to be truck drivers or gas station attendants or factory workers. There was suddenly this possibility to actually make a killing and get your own mansion—which is very American."

T-Bone Burnett
*Written in my Soul: Rock's Great Songwriters Talk about Creating their Music*

"I knew what I wanted to do and I knew that I had to do it or else I'd be stuck. I wasn't going to raise cotton and I knew Lubbock had a dismal view of musicians, even though there was a great music thing going on there."

Musician Joe Ely, on leaving Lubbock as a career move
*The Dallas Morning News High Profile*

"You'll do anything to get out of West Texas . . . . It's either music or pull cotton for the rest of your life."

Waylon Jennings, 1995
*Buddy Holly, A Biography*

 ☆ ☆ ☆

"I had always loved music, but I had no illusions about making a career out of it . . . . My drive was to be a musician . . . and to stay away from anything resembling a full-time job."

Musician Lyle Lovett, 1992
*Texas Monthly*

 ☆ ☆ ☆

"My father had worked in the oil fields. And I knew there'd always be a demand for geologists . . . I wanted to get a diploma in case I didn't make it in the music business."

Musician Roy Orbison, explaining why he majored in geology at North Texas State University
*Dark Star: The Roy Orbison Story*

33

34

"I would have loved to have been a professional rodeo competitor. But when it came time for me to choose a career, country music seemed to have a better future. Looking back, I guess I made the right decision, but rodeo will always be an important part of my life."

Country musician George Strait
*Country America*

"I was at North Texas the same time he was. I was playing guitar but had to leave school to go to work with my daddy for a while. Pat used school to help his career. They even let him out of college to tour. So, in that respect, he inspired me to get off my duff and get to work."

Roy Orbison, who was inspired by Pat Boone while attending North Texas State University
*Dark Star: The Roy Orbison Story*

"I'm gonna go on doing what I'm gonna do, and if people pick up on it, that's wonderful. And if they don't, I can always drive a tractor."

West Texas musician Butch Hancock
*Prairie Nights to Neon Lights: The Story of Country Music in West Texas*

"All musicians are surprised to last more than a year in this business."

Billy Gibbons, ZZ Top guitarist
*ZZ Top—Recycling The Blues*

"Buddy was head-to-toe music and he really didn't have any other interests. But he did like to draw and design. In fact, he said once that if he couldn't be a success in music, he'd like to be an engineer or a draftsman."

Maria Elena Holly, Buddy Holly's widow
*The Buddy Holly Story*

☆ ☆ ☆

"It's my life. It's everything. I have been gifted with something, and if I don't take it to its fullest extent, I might as well be farting in the bushes."

Stevie Ray Vaughan, on his career in music
*Stevie Ray Vaughan: Caught In the Crossfire*

35

36

"I knew this kid is either gonna become a multi-millionaire, or he's gonna starve in the pits. He wasn't that smart intellectually, but when it came to music, that guitar was his whole life."

Musician Christian Plicque, on Stevie Ray Vaughan, his childhood friend
*Stevie Ray Vaughan: Caught In the Crossfire*

"Musicians never stop paying their dues, unless they quit playing. And I can't quit playing. I don't know what else I'd do. I wouldn't be happy, I know that."

Steve Fromholz
*The Improbable Rise of Redneck Rock*

"I know that writing pop music as a whole is a some-what shallow occupation. It's something I don't want to do all my life . . . . The pop field is given more credit and importance than it deserves. I think it has its place. It can be a very beautiful thing, I've enjoyed being a songwriter. Gershwin was a very good song-writer, but Gershwin also did other things . . . . I'm still just a songwriter, but I'd also like to be like him."

Country-pop musician Michael Martin Murphey, 1974
*The Improbable Rise of Redneck Rock*

"I'm not trying to be a country singer. For that matter, I'm not trying to be a rock 'n' roll singer, or a folksinger, or a pop singer. I'm a singer, and I'm a songwriter. I try to write songs lyrically in a way that people anywhere in the world can relate to them."

Pop/country musician John Denver
*Take Me Home*

"Maybe your songs did mean something to some. If so, that's fine, but still you have to aspire to something higher. Otherwise, you'll be a pop songwriter the rest of your life, and you'll always be trying to come up with one more top-forty hit."

Michael Martin Murphey, 1974
*The Improbable Rise of Redneck Rock*

"Business-wise, Buddy really had it together. Creatively, he did it all—wrote songs, played guitar, sang."

Holly fan Bill Griggs
*Texas Monthly*

37

38

"I just wanted to write songs. I never thought of myself as a great singer.  Every time I'd start to think, well, maybe I do want to be a singer, I'd go hear someone like Emmylou Harris, and I'd think, now that's a singer."

Nanci Griffith
*The Dallas Morning News High Profile*

"All my best songs took only half an hour to write . . . I generally write the bare bones of the song then leave it for two or three months."

Roy Orbison
*Only The Lonely*

☆ ☆ ☆

"Basically, we're on stage . . . we're acting. I mean we're not singing about reality all the time . . . . If I've got a fifteen-year career, who wants to hear me sing about how great my marriage is for fifteen years?"

Tracy Byrd
*Sherman Democrat*

"If you're gonna sing a sad song, or ballad, you've got to have lived it yourself."

George Jones
*You're the Reason our Kids are Ugly and Other Gems of Country Music Wisdom*

"I live my songs too strongly."

George Jones
*You're the Reason our Kids are Ugly and Other Gems of Country Music Wisdom*

"We're not gonna see a new record from me for at least a year. Rome wasn't built in a day. Peoria wasn't built in a day. But I've been working on songs for two or three movies."

Don Henley, 1986
*Rolling Stone*

"I've been plodding along like the tortoise for all these years. I mean, I've only made three albums in this decade."

Don Henley, 1989
*Rolling Stone*

"What I always liked to do was be the guitar player. Somewhere along the way, I started being the singer. I'm not sure how that happened."

Willie Nelson
*Country Musicians*

"When I was fifteen, I went in the back of the house to play my guitar and sing a little bit. And I could only play what I knew, I couldn't think of any innovations, or any other chords. I made the decision then not to be a guitar player, but to use the instrument as an accompaniment to my singing."

Roy Orbison
*Dark Star: The Roy Orbison Story*

40

"There wasn't a whole lot of difference between dealing with a room full of kindergarteners and a barroom full of drunks."

Nanci Griffith, a former teacher
*You're the Reason our Kids are Ugly and Other Gems of Country Music Wisdom*

"It's just more songs by me."

Lyle Lovett, describing his new record album, 1992
*Rolling Stone*

"We were hoping to maybe have a moderate hit, so we could keep making records. At the very least, I just wanted an album to give to my mother."

Musician Christopher Cross, reflecting on his 1980 Grammy-winning album
*The Dallas Morning News*

41

"There's really nothing to say about me or the band that's interesting. We're just a bunch of normal kids who lucked into being a successful band."

Edie Brickell, leader of Edie Brickell and the New Bohemians
*Rolling Stone*

"You will have to go out there and hit a home run with every single you release. There are so many artists out there that do mediocre material but can sing. And it doesn't matter how good you sing, how many notes you can hit, how high or how low you can go, you have to make people believe what you're singing. You can't fool the public all the time."

Clay Walker
*The Dallas Morning News Weekend Guide*

"When they called 'em rock and roll pioneers, they were talking about the music. But that pretty much described the living conditions, too."

Waylon Jennings, on his days touring with Buddy Holly
*You're the Reason our Kids are Ugly and Other Gems of Country Music Wisdom*

"People don't realize today how the managers and agents dictate the lives of the performers. The more you need somebody to handle your money and affairs the more separated you become from the whole thing of getting up and playing for people that come to pay money."

Country musician Willis Alan Ramsey, 1974
*The Improbable Rise of Redneck Rock*

"Playing music is not good for a marriage relationship at all. Our kind of life is hard on women. I have to do it though. I couldn't sit back and be a songwriter or studio musician. I enjoy the crowds, I love to work with audiences."

Rusty Wier
*The Improbable Rise of Redneck Rock*

"I've been married nearly my whole life, and I've been a road musician nearly my whole life. And I know those two are incompatible."

Willie Nelson
*Willie: An Autobiography*

44

"The honky-tonk environment is definitely to be avoided if you intend to make a living while staying away from beer and whiskey and dope."

Willie Nelson
*Willie: An Autobiography*

"It's never too late. I've decided to be a fifty-five-year-old, middle-aged sex symbol."

Waylon Jennings
*Talkin' Country: Down-Home Philosophy and Advice from Country's Biggest Stars*

☆ ☆ ☆

"You don't even know what you're doing until about forty-five. And I don't think—as a musician—you really hit your peak until you're about sixty. Let me go out like Dizzy Gillespie. Let me be around and play."

Rock/pop musician Steve Miller, on aging
*Rock Talk*

"I used to say that as soon as we have a gold record, that's certainly one of the signs of the Apocalypse that David Koresh was looking for. Something is definitely wrong with society when the Butthole Surfers become popular."

King Coffey, drummer for the Austin underground band Butthole Surfers, after their 1993 album sold 300,000 copies
*Texas Monthly, June 1996*

"Don't write us old-timers off. We ain't dead yet."

George Jones
*Pride: The Charley Pride Story*

"I sing better now, I play better now. I'm much better than I was in 1976, 1986, or 1994. I would expect my peak of creativity will be in my sixties."

Steve Miller, 1995
*Sherman Democrat*

45

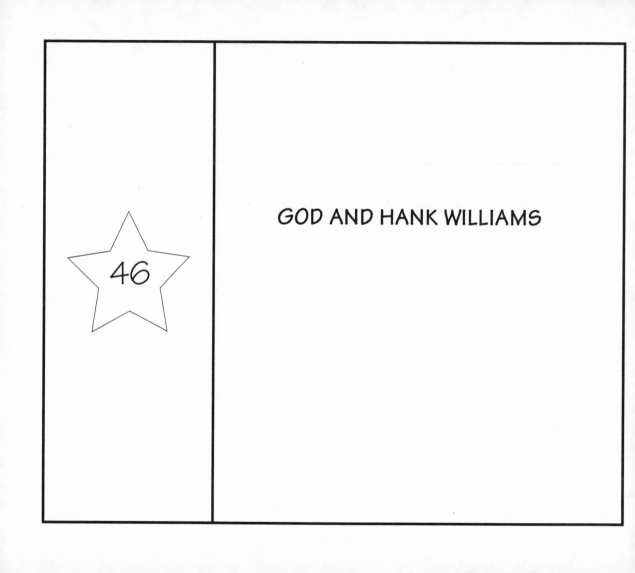

**46**

GOD AND HANK WILLIAMS

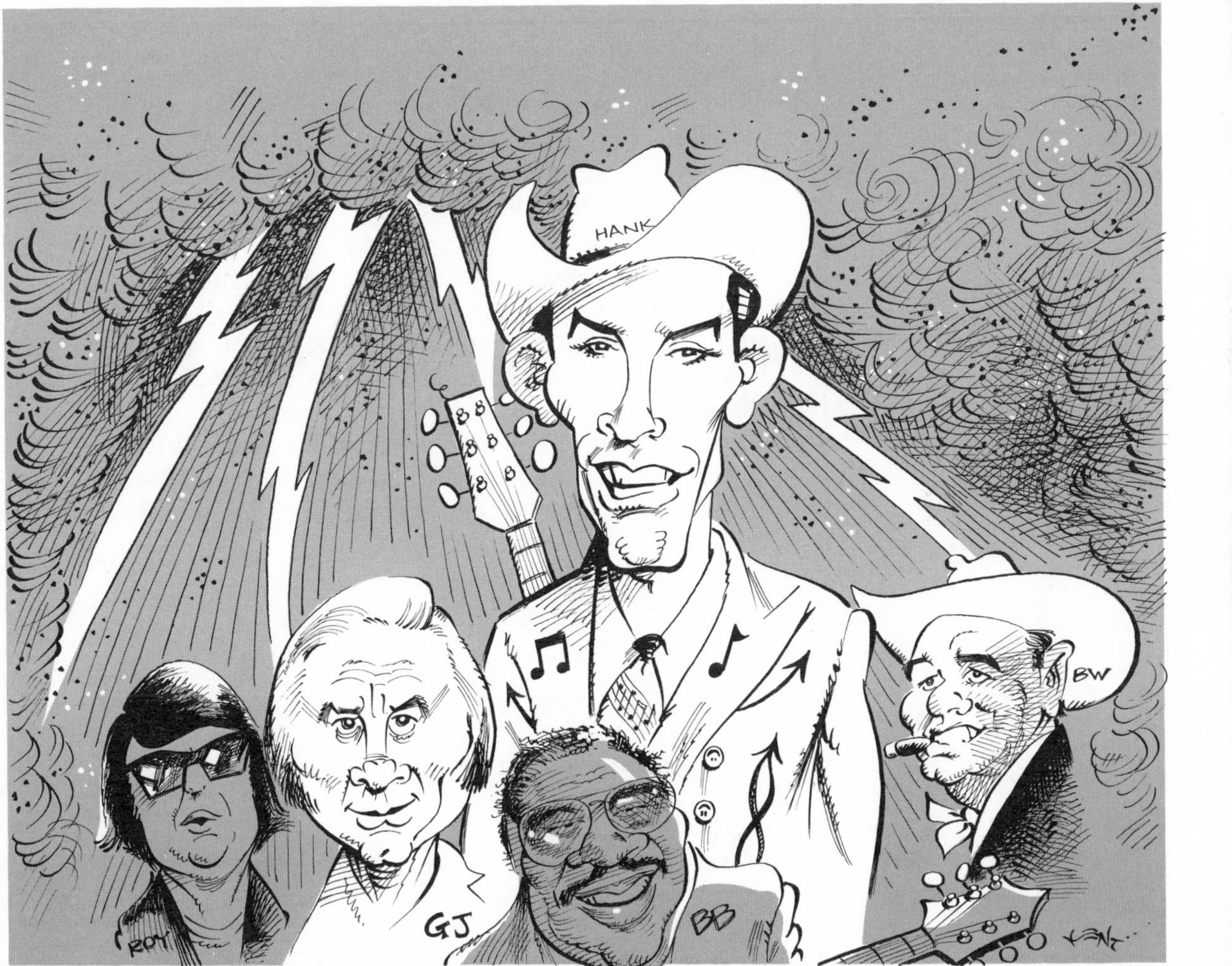
HANK
ROY
GJ
BB
BW

48

Most recording artists who have achieved any sort of fame are quick to cite their musical influences and give due credit. Many a Texas musician was influenced by the music they grew up with in church, radio airplay, and phonograph records.

Heading this "roots" list are the likes of western swing pioneer Bob Wills, smooth singing Roy Orbison, rock 'n' roll pacesetter Buddy Holly, and such blues guitarists/performers as T-Bone Walker, B. B. King, Jimmy Reed, Muddy Waters, Bobby Bland, and Ray Charles.

But perhaps Texas-born George Jones put it best: "I have two heroes. God and Hank Williams. Make sure you hold up the very best as your ideals."

"At least the first forty songs we wrote were Buddy Holly-influenced."

Paul McCartney of the Beatles
*Prairie Nights to Neon Lights: The Story of Country Music in West Texas*

"When Elvis came through Lubbock, we were still in high school and Buddy really got hung up on Elvis. We started the next day after he left town doing his songs. I had a Martin D-28 and Buddy had a Stratocaster and we traded because the Martin was the kind of guitar Elvis played and Buddy wanted to be like Elvis."

Sonny Curtis
*Prairie Nights to Neon Lights: The Story of Country Music in West Texas*

 ☆ ☆ ☆

"Here was a white guy who came on stage with a guitar. I had been interested in singing before that, but a guy playing guitar wasn't that cool until Elvis came along. After that, if you held a guitar, or even looked like you were going to play a guitar, the girls would scream at you. So I got a guitar."

Dallas rockabilly performer Ronnie Dawson on being influenced by Elvis Presley
*The Dallas Morning News High Profile*

49

**50**

"The music of the late fifties and early sixties when music was at that root level—that for me is meaningful music. The singers and musicians I grew up with transcend nostalgia—Buddy Holly and Johnny Ace are just as valid to me today as then."

Musician Bob Dylan, 1974
*Newsweek*

"I turned a deaf ear on the rock-and-roll craze that was sweeping the nation back in the late 1950s and early 1960s. Guys like Elvis Presley, Ricky Nelson, Pat Boone, Buddy Holly, Roy Orbison—all that stuff meant nothing to me."

Senior pro golfer Robert Landers
*Greener Pastures: An Incredible Journey from the Farm to the Fairway*

☆ ☆ ☆

"I began wearing glasses when I was thirteen to copy Buddy Holly."

Rock musician Elton John
*The Buddy Holly Story*

"Buddy Holly was the first and last person I ever really idolized as a kid."

Pop singer/songwriter Don McLean
*Buddy Holly: A Biography*

 ☆ ☆ ☆

"Buddy Holly was my very first favorite and my inspiration to go into the music business. I still think he is among the very best. He was different, exciting, and inimitable!"

George Harrison of the Beatles
*Buddy Holly: A Biography*

☆ ☆ ☆

"I always loved Roy. I looked up to the way he was, admired the way he handled himself. That aloofness he had influenced me profoundly. It was the way he carried himself, you know, with this benign dignity. His music was always more important than the media."

Rock 'n' roller Neil Young, on Roy Orbison
*Small Talk, Big Names—40 Years of Rock Quotes*

51

"From watching Roy, I learned how to sing a dramatic ballad."

Mick Jagger of the Rolling Stones, on Roy Orbison
*Rolling Stone*

"I grew up on country music in Lubbock in the forties. I listened to Little Jimmy Dickens and Hank Williams and Patti Page, and an awful lot of Bob Wills. I moved to Fort Worth in 1951, and then in the early fifties I started listening to the doo-wop singers: the Turbans, the Lamplighters, the Penguins . . ."

Blues/country musician Delbert McClinton
*The New Country Music Encyclopedia*

"I didn't grow up with Bob Wills and Hank Thompson. I grew up with the people that grew up with them, like Merle Haggard and Gene Watson and George Strait. It's kind of like your grandfather . . . I never gave those older guys like Bob Wills any thought, but I'm starting to think about them now."

Clint Black
*The New Country Music Encyclopedia*

52

"There is only one George Strait, and it felt odd to be compared to him, even though he is my biggest influence."

Tracy Byrd, 1995
*The Dallas Morning News*

"These new country stars seem to pop out of the recording studio devoid of emotional heritage. They're big stars in a week. I'm sure Garth Brooks is a very nice guy, but the people who go to see him could just as easily [have] been at Disneyland and would have liked it just as much. I've taken to calling him the anti-Hank."

Kinky Friedman, comparing contemporary stars to Hank Williams,1993
*Texas Monthly*

☆ ☆ ☆

"Junior Brown is the greatest thing to come to country music since Hank, Sr. I've made that statement before, and I've looked back on it in context, and I still think it's true. He has created a whole new style with his guit steel."

Dallas club owner John Bailey, on country musician Junior Brown and his steel guitar, 1996
*The Dallas Morning News*

53

**54**

"I had been exposed to other music—blues and gospel, mostly—but Roy Acuff, Ernest Tubb, and Hank Williams came into our house . . . . It was natural that my taste in music would lean in their direction. I sang along with those guys, memorized their songs, and country music just grew inside me."

Charley Pride, explaining the influence of radio on his style
*Pride: The Charley Pride Story*

"There was just something about the way Tubb sang, what he'd put into a song, his whole style and the style of the band. We were listening to rock and roll back then; you were square if you didn't. But Ernest Tubb had something that I liked."

Junior Brown, on Ernest Tubb
*The Met*

"He was a very nice guy and was very supportive of the younger singers. This was during a period where a lot of bands were taking the steel and the fiddles out of the music. Ernest Tubb was one who wanted the younger people to not water country music so far down it was gone."

Junior Brown, on Ernest Tubb
*The Met*

 ☆ ☆ ☆

"He made it possible for cowboy or country singers to get employment on radio stations. He was responsible for the sale of more guitars than any other man. He made the value of country songs and records into a commercial product that since then has been recognized as an important part of the music industry. He made it possible for hillbilly entertainers to play theatres and first rate entertainment places."

Country musician Ernest Tubb, on Jimmie Rodgers, the legendary blues yodeler of the 1930s
*Jimmie Rodgers: The Life and Times of America's Blue Yodeler*

55

56

"The Eagles live on the charts. But George Jones, Lefty Frizzell, and Hank Williams live in the heart."

Kinky Friedman
*Austin City Limits*

☆ ☆ ☆

"I loved Lefty Frizzell, Bob Wills, Floyd Tillman, Leon Payne, Hank Williams, Bill Boyd, and the Cowboy Ramblers. . . . A fellow called Ernest Tubb landed on the Grand Ole Opry, and the search was all over for me—I had found my first singing hero."

Willie Nelson, on discovering Ernest Tubb in 1943
*Willie: An Autobiography*

☆ ☆ ☆

"Actually, it was good for me to have grown up in West Texas, because I wasn't caught up in any musical influence. Except for Bob Wills' western swing, there wasn't any musical influence. So when rock came along, I was ready for it."

Roy Orbison
*Dark Star: The Roy Orbison Story*

"Bob Wills is still the king. . . . Bob Wills was such a big star that he looked like he was made out of wax. He was almost like an animation. Watching him move around, I thought: This guy ain't real. He had a presence about him. He had an aura so strong it just stunned people."

Willie Nelson
*Willie: An Autobiography*

"Bob Wills taught me how to be a bandleader and how to be a star."

Willie Nelson
*Willie: An Autobiography*

"People are going to buy Willie Nelson records for the rest of their lives, and so will their children."

Nelson's stage manager Randy "Poodie" Locke
*Willie: An Autobiography*

"I love traditional country music. I grew up with it and love what it does for me. I try to write and perform it. But then there's this side of me that loves Bob Dylan and the Beatles, Tom Petty and the Heartbreakers and Bruce Springsteen."

Country singer/songwriter Radney Foster
*The Dallas Morning News*

"Where I come from in Texas, I grew up hearing blues and rhythm 'n' blues. I have to give full tribute to black music for teaching me an awful lot and giving me a lot of pleasure."

Boz Scaggs
*Sherman Democrat*

"We all loved Elvis and Hank Williams, but I think Wilson had the biggest influence on me. I couldn't believe what he could do with his voice . . . I listened to him on the radio and on records every chance I got, wondering how anyone could sing that good."

B. J. Thomas, on Jackie Wilson
*Home Where I Belong*

58

"Back in Port Arthur, I'd heard some Leadbelly records, and, well, if the blues syndrome is true, I guess it's true about me. So I began listening to blues and folk music. I bought Bessie Smith records, and Odetta and Billie Holliday."

Rock musician Janis Joplin
*Janis Joplin—Piece of my Heart*

"My earliest heroes were Ray Charles and Bobby Bland, T-Bone Walker and B. B. King."

Boz Scaggs
*The Dallas Morning News*

"I grew up with a lot of R and B, too—I think that Big Joe Turner and Hank Williams come from the same honky-tonk place."

Rodney Crowell
*The New Country Music Encyclopedia*

59

"I grew up on straight soul music. I'm a self-indulgent singer. So we split. I wanted to do more soul. The band wanted to jam, so much like The Grateful Dead."

Edie Brickell, on the break-up of her band, Edie Brickell and the New Bohemians, 1995
*Parade Magazine*

"My influences as a singer have been Tina Turner, her energy, but mainly I liked the low-down blues guys that didn't have beautiful voices: J. B. Hutto, Frankie Lee Sims, Dr. Ross, Etta James, Big Mama Thornton, who I got to know a little bit out on the West Coast. Magic Sam was a real favorite of mine."

Angela Strehli
*Meeting the Blues: The Rise of the Texas Sound*

"T-Bone Walker was probably my favorite of Texas people. Even though I don't sound a whole lot like him, I probably learned more from him than anybody . . . I always thought that I always was more influenced by the music in Chicago and the Delta than the Texas music that was actually around me . . . I didn't really think of myself as a Texas musician until later."

Johnny Winter
*Meeting the Blues: The Rise of the Texas Sound*

☆ ☆ ☆

"When I came up, T-Bone Walker was my biggest influence. I refer to him as the grandfather of the blues guitar because he was one of the first to play with an electric instrument. T-Bone expressed his feelings through different melodies played on the electric guitar like no one else. As far as I'm concerned he originated it, and after him, as far as Texas was concerned, was Gatemouth Brown."

Blues guitarist Joe Hughes
*Meeting the Blues: The Rise of the Texas Sound*

61

"The first time I ever heard a boogie-woogie piano was the first time I went to church. That was the Holy Ghost Church in Dallas. . . . That's where the music was."

Legendary blues player T-Bone Walker
*Texas Rhythm, Texas Rhyme*

"I just love B. B. King; he plays guitar so good I don't even want to talk about him. . . . But I tell you who I really love—ol' Jimmy Reed. Someday they're going to realize just how great he was."

Waylon Jennings
*Country Musicians*

"In a way I'm more influenced by the Chicago sound, Muddy Waters, Magic Sam, Buddy Guy, B. B. I like that harmonica a lot; Little Walter, Robert Jr. Lockwood, Luther Tucker, they're all big influences, too. I kind of pulled something from everybody. I do what I do and go on. I don't think about it too much."

Blues guitarist Anson Funderburgh
*Meeting the Blues: The Rise of the Texas Sound*

"I like to think that when I play the guitar it sounds like Dallas. That's where I learned everything, and all of the people I saw were playing here. I suppose it's a crazy way of putting it. I heard everyone that influenced me, either live or on the radio, KNOK or 'Cat's Caravan' on WRR."

Blues guitarist Jimmie Vaughan
*Meeting the Blues: The Rise of the Texas Sound*

"In my style I borrowed a lot of things: Freddie King, B. B. King, Lightnin' Hopkins, T-Bone Walker. I may have my own approach, but it's a Texas guitar sound."

Jimmie Vaughan
*Meeting the Blues: The Rise of the Texas Sound*

"I've never really thought there really was much of a Texas style. If there is anything that really stands out, there are so many different influences in Texas guitar players. You just can't say they sound the same way."

Johnny Winter
*Meeting the Blues: The Rise of the Texas Sound*

63

64

"But my biggest influence has been my brother, Jimmie, because of probably all the other influences he made possible for me to have. Those people included Freddie King, B. B. King, Albert King, Lonnie Mack."

Stevie Ray Vaughan
*Meeting the Blues: The Rise of the Texas Sound*

☆ ☆ ☆

"A lot of my ideas came from hearing people like Jeff Beck and Clapton, who I first heard at the same time I started listening to Howlin' Wolf and Muddy Waters and all those guys, when I was real young. I think every guitar player who came up in Texas played Jeff's 'Boogie.'"

Stevie Ray Vaughan
*Rolling Stone*

☆ ☆ ☆

"[Jimi] Hendrix did everybody a favor by showing us you can put all these styles of music together and make it work. . . . I'll probably put a Hendrix song on every record I ever make 'cause I like him so much."

Stevie Ray Vaughan
*Stevie Ray: Soul to Soul*

"If it hadn't been for Stevie, there wouldn't be a market for Colin James or Jeff Healey or Robert Cray. They wouldn't have big record deals. He made the blues popular again in the eighties, and inspired a lot of young guys to go back and listen to the masters."

Danny Thorpe, a friend of Vaughan's
*Stevie Ray: Soul to Soul*

"From the outside, it seemed like all there used to be was progressive country. But we all knew there was something different bubbling under the surface, like Jimmie Vaughan and the Fabulous Thunderbirds. I play the guitar the way I do because of him. He has influenced me just like Willie has influenced my songwriting."

Lee Roy Parnell, on the country music sound in Austin, 1994
*Texas Monthly*

66

"I listened to everything from the Jackson 5 to the Carpenters. I graduated high school in 1976, and I was into the disco thing. . . . That's why my voice is maybe a little different than what is out there. When you listen to everything from James Ingram to Luther Vandross to Boz Scaggs, some of that has to rub off on you."

Country musician Neal McCoy, 1995
*The Dallas Morning News Weekend Guide*

"As a child, I wanted to grow up and be a Cindy Walker, a Harlan Howard, or a Buddy Holly . . . Loretta Lynn just blew me away. I wanted to be somebody who wrote songs for great voices."

Nanci Griffith
*The Dallas Morning News High Profile*

"I'm just now starting to develop my own style. I pulled some of what I do from various influences. Now when people hear me, I hope they think, hope it sounds like me. I don't really want to sound like someone else."

Anson Funderburgh
*Meeting the Blues: The Rise of the Texas Sound*

"I see my music going every which way. The reason I say that is because I never felt like it was confined. I never thought it was anything but what comes naturally. It's country music, R and B music, a combination of everything I've heard all my life. I've been influenced by everybody I ever heard, but I've never tried to copy anybody."

Delbert McClinton
*Meeting the Blues: The Rise of the Texas Sound*

"I prefer to go in my own direction and let someone follow me."

Country musician Roger Miller
*You're the Reason our Kids are Ugly and Other Gems of Country Music Wisdom*

"Patsy Cline was one of the first country music artists I listened to. I love her music. She's been a big influence on me."

Country singer LeAnn Rimes, who at age 13 had a hit single "Blue," 1996
*Country Weekly*

67

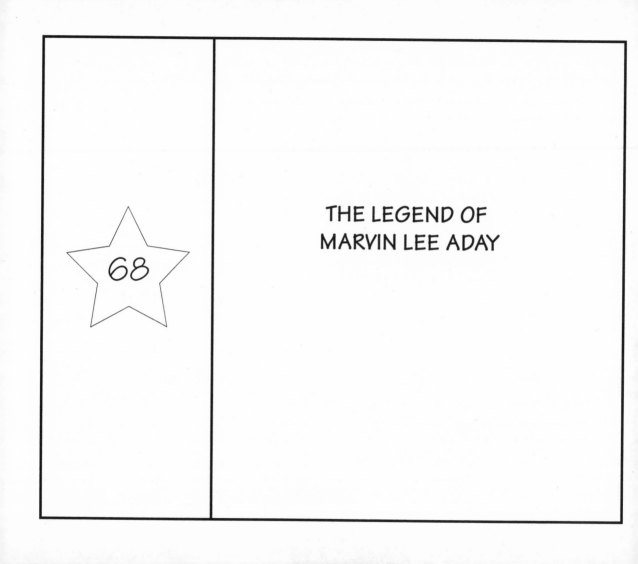

68

# THE LEGEND OF
# MARVIN LEE ADAY

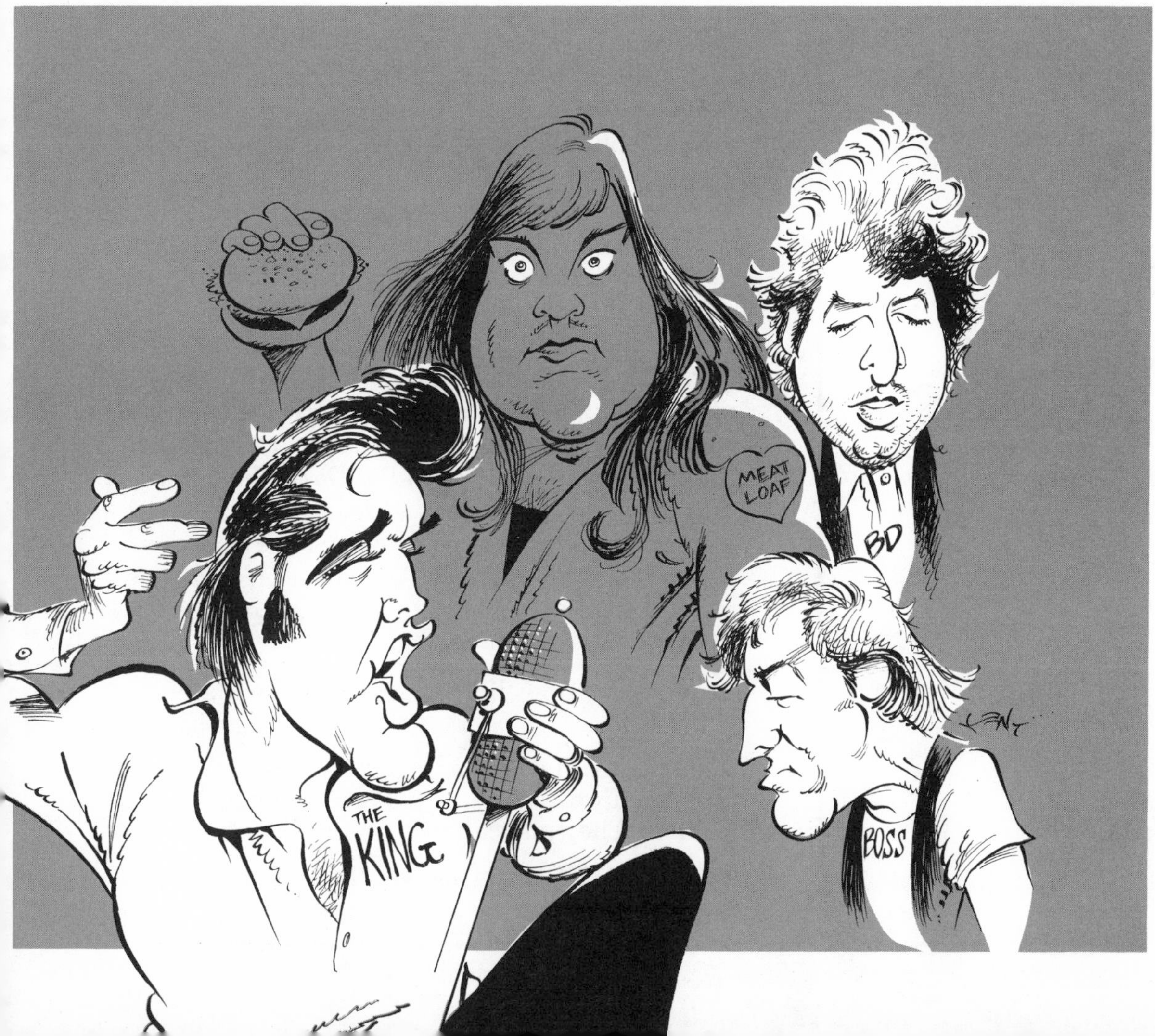
MEAT LOAF
BD
THE KING
BOSS

70

Over the years, most musicians acquire an image and reputation, whether it be good, bad, or ugly. This image—many times cultivated by an artist and/or management—is critical to how the musician is perceived.

Take the case of rock 'n' roller Marvin Lee Aday, who attended Dallas's Thomas Jefferson High School. Now known to the world as Meat Loaf, he burst onto the musical scene in 1977 with a thirty-million-selling album entitled *Bat Out of Hell*. The intense, heavyset Mr. Loaf excelled with rock songs performed in an almost operatic or theatrical method. (After a long, dry spell, he reemerged with similar success in 1993 with *Bat Out of Hell II: Back Into Hell*.)

Just how Marvin Lee Aday came to be known as Meat Loaf is, well, unclear. At last count, there were seven different versions as to the origin of the nickname. Here are three examples:

**Question**: "How did you get the nickname Meat Loaf?"

**Meat Loaf:** "I was playing grade school football. I was ten years old and weighed 200 pounds. They just called me Meat Loaf."

**Question:** "How did you get the nickname Meat Loaf?"

**Meat Loaf:** "One night when I was in high school, everybody was going to a card game, and I didn't have any money. So this guy Billy turned to me and, as a joke, said, 'I'll give you a hundred bucks if you let the front wheel of this Volkswagon roll over your head.' I thought about it, said, OK, lay down, and they undid the brake. Then I got the $100, went to the game and won $2,000." To which his friends said, "You've gotta have meat loaf for brains to do that!"

**Question:** "How did you get the nickname Meat Loaf?"

**Meat Loaf:** "When I was five years old, my parents and I were flying with Chip Piper, of Piper Aircraft, in a Beechcraft. There was an emergency landing. It was at night. I was only five, but I managed to wake up in a cave. This was in Wyoming. I was found the next day by Lamar Hunt. He was elk hunting. I was in a state of shock, and the only thing I could say was 'meat loaf.' From that point on, everyone called me Meat Loaf."

And finally, Mrs. Meat Loaf, a.k.a. Leslie Aday, told *The Dallas Morning News* that she is not even sure of the truth. "I think it is probably rather painful,

71

the true story," she said. "Can you imagine being a prepubescent child and weighing 200 pounds?"

"Bob's a party waiting to happen. There's no truth to the rumor that the date on his carton has expired."

Kinky Friedman, on Bob Dylan, 1993
*Texas Monthly*

72

"Good musician, but bloody obnoxious. He makes more enemies than friends."

Rolling Stone member Bill Wyman, on rock musician Stephen Stills
*Small Talk, Big Names—40 Years of Rock Quotes*

☆ ☆ ☆

"When I go onstage, I put those sunglasses on, and I'm the Gangster Of Love. I take the Ray-Bans off, and I'm Steve. And really that's pretty much the way my life works. I'm always amazed at all those guys who work so hard offstage at being so groovy. It's so hard—takes so much makeup and hair."

Steve Miller, 1993
*Rolling Stone*

"James has a gift. He's only twenty-seven, but he writes songs like he's lived 150 years."

Rock musician John Cougar Mellencamp, on James McMurtry, 1989
*Rolling Stone*

"Freddy is one of the unmistakable voices of Texas music, much like Roy Orbison and Buddy Holly. He has been bending genres to fit his unique style for many, many years."

Casey Monahan, director of the Texas Music Office in the governor's office, on Freddy Fender
*Sherman Democrat*

☆ ☆ ☆

"Roy's voice just came through the radio and touched parts of you that other people didn't reach."

George Harrison, on Roy Orbison
*Rolling Stone*

73

74

"When you were trying to make a girl fall in love with you, it took roses, the Ferris wheel, and Roy Orbison."

Musician Tom Waits
*Rolling Stone*

"Roy was an opera singer. He had the greatest voice."

Bob Dylan
*Rolling Stone*

"The nearest thing to Roy—there's nothing like it in rock music—the nearest thing is Verdi and Puccini in grand opera. But growing up in Wink, Texas, there isn't much opera around."

Will Jennings, a songwriting partner of Roy Orbison
*Rolling Stone*

"If you play his records, his records do not sound like oldies records."

Rock musician Bruce Springsteen, on Roy Orbison
*Rolling Stone*

"Caruso in sunglasses and a leather jacket."

Tom Waits, on Roy Orbison
*Rolling Stone*

"I started using sunglasses in Alabama. I was going to do a show with Patsy Cline and Bobby Vee and I left my clear glasses on the plane. I only had the sunshades, and I was quite embarrassed to go on stage with them, but I did it."

Roy Orbison, on his trademark sunglasses
*Off the Record: An Oral History of Popular Music*

"Everyone at one time or another tries to write a Roy Orbison song. Mine was 'Don't Let the Sun Go Down On Me.'"

Composer Bernie Taupin
*Dark Star: The Roy Orbison Story*

75

76

"I remember Roy minded his own business, stayed in his place. He always kept to himself, pretty much. He might come by just to say hello, hug your neck real nice, and get out of your hair. He was that kind of person. He was a pretty nice guy, wasn't he? And he sang his butt off."

Musician Jerry Lee Lewis, on touring with Orbison
*Dark Star: The Roy Orbison Story*

"Roy was always very suppressed, a very private guy. He enjoyed his privacy but he also wanted to be recognized. He was contradictory and torn."

Drummer Paul Garrison
*Dark Star: The Roy Orbison Story*

"As a musician-singer-artist Roy was without parallel. He was just the greatest. You know, of course, that he was Elvis Presley's favorite singer. He certainly was one of mine. The thing about Roy was that while he influenced so many people through the years, nobody could ever do what he did exactly. Very few singers have the range that he had."

Musician Duane Eddy
*Dark Star: The Roy Orbison Story*

"I am blessed with a terrific voice. It's a God-given thing, but I sang a lot as a teenager and there were no barometers around. I was the only guy singing and playing guitar in my area. If you learn to play different songs for dances and presentations, and you get a band together, you just naturally get better."

Roy Orbison
*Off the Record: An Oral History of Popular Music*

"I've always been in love with my voice. It was fascinating. I liked the sound of it, I liked making it sing, making a voice ring, and I just kept doing it."

Roy Orbison
*Dark Star: The Roy Orbison Story*

"I can't believe the power that I have behind my voice. Usually you can tell the voice is good when you talk and it feels like there's a little speaker in there that reinforces it."

Country musician Freddy Fender
*Sherman Democrat*

78

"I've been blessed with a voice and I want to use it well, but I'll not take every performance so seriously that I judge my character by it."

B. J. Thomas
*Home Where I Belong*

"I'm a country boy made good on the music scene, a drug addict saved by grace."

B. J. Thomas, referring to his status as a born-again Christian
*Home Where I Belong*

"Johnny Ace was the first black guy I know of, way before Ray Charles, who could sing country-tainted songs—blues and country together. He carried a song, and it was a feeling you couldn't forget. He had teardrops in his voice."

Huey P. Meaux
*Rolling Stone*

"If we could all sound like we wanted to, we'd all sound like George Jones."

Waylon Jennings
*Texas Monthly*

☆ ☆ ☆

"I've never talked to a country music person whose favorite singer wasn't George Jones."

Country musician Tom T. Hall
*Ragged but Right: The Life and Times of George Jones*

☆ ☆ ☆

"When you hear George Jones sing you are hearing a man who takes a song and makes it a work of art—always. He has a remarkable voice that flows out of him effortlessly, and quietly, but with an edge that comes from the stormy part of the heart. In the South we call it 'high lonesome.' I think it is popularly called 'soul.'"

Country musician Emmylou Harris
*Ragged but Right: The Life and Times of George Jones*

79

"I can say, without hesitation, that George Jones is the greatest country music singer who has ever lived."

Buddy Killen, president of Tree International Music Publishing
*Ragged but Right: The Life and Times of George Jones*

"George Jones is king."

Country musician Garth Brooks, 1994
*Texas Monthly*

"He's the Shakespeare of country music."

Tom T. Hall, on Willie Nelson
*Austin City Limits*

"Willie Nelson's the greatest songwriter who's ever been, I really believe that."

Waylon Jennings
*The Outlaws: Revolution in Country Music*

"If there is one thing I have known I am good at since I was old enough to catch the first thoughts and sounds that passed through me, it is songwriting. There are a million things I can't do, but songwriting I can do."

Willie Nelson
*Willie: An Autobiography*

"A carved-in-granite samurai poet warrior gypsy guitar-pickin' wild man with a heart as big as Texas."

Kris Kristofferson, on Willie Nelson
*Parade Magazine*

"I knew right off Willie would be a star because everybody was listening to him and feeling his magic. I damn sure felt it—kind of like the pull of a magnet. There's two people I know of who have magic that strong—Willie Nelson and Billy Graham."

Casino owner Bennie Binion
*Willie: An Autobiography*

81

82

"Willie was the old one, Waylon was the mean one,
and Jerry Jeff was the drunk one, David Allen Coe
was the cussin' one, and I was the wild one."

Ray Wylie Hubbard, on the outlaws of country music, 1993
*D Magazine*

"Willie's the only person I know to be arrested for
sleeping under the influence."

Waylon Jennings, after police found marijuana in Willie Nelson's car
while Willie was asleep (charges were later dropped)
*The Dallas Morning News*

☆ ☆ ☆

"Hell, I ain't no great guitar player. I just play my
stuff. I'm very self-conscious about my guitar playing
for some reason. I'm a singer, I never practice on my
guitar."

Waylon Jennings
*Country Music*

"Waylon's idea of being low-key is to drive an orange Cadillac convertible with a white top and a Continental kit on the back."

Tompall Glaser
*Willie: An Autobiography*

☆ ☆ ☆

"He was the closest thing Austin had to Hank Williams."

Author Jan Reid, on Jerry Jeff Walker
*The Improbable Rise of Redneck Rock*

☆ ☆ ☆

"The most famous musician in Austin when I got there was Jerry Jeff Walker."

Willie Nelson
*Willie: An Autobiography*

☆ ☆ ☆

"Kris is, of course, one of the best songwriters of all time. He shows more soul when he blows his nose than the ordinary person does at his honeymoon dance."

Willie Nelson, on Kris Kristofferson
*Willie: An Autobiography*

84

"I like to look for songs that I thought the writer lived or fooled me into thinking he lived. For instance, Kristofferson has always been one of my favorite writers, and here's a guy that if he didn't live every song he ever wrote, he fooled me."

Country musician Collin Raye
*The Dallas Morning News*

"Some writers listen to so much music, there's no room left for their own writing. My writing comes in spurts . . . I want my songs to come from me rather than somewhere else."

Junior Brown
*The Met*

"I don't know why anyone would want to hear me. I sound like a damned frog."

Kris Kristofferson
*You're the Reason our Kids are Ugly and Other Gems of Country Music Wisdom*

"Rap is from the streets and I'm from the streets. That's why a lot of people accept me."

Vanilla Ice, 1990
*People Magazine*

"Garth Brooks is the Vanilla Ice of country music."

*Rolling Stone*

"Sometimes I feel like I'm not paying enough attention to what's going on—all of a sudden Garth Brooks is the biggest thing in the world, and I still didn't know who he was . . . I mean, I'm happy for him, more power to him, but I don't see where it's coming from."

Musician Delbert McClinton
*The New Country Music Encyclopedia*

85

**86**

"Everybody loves Junior. Because he's the best of both worlds. He's got some of today's rock influences, but his feet are firmly planted in true country. He's not that manufactured Nashville stuff. He combines every influence in the book."

Mike Snider of the Sons of Hermann Hall concert arena, on Junior Brown
*The Met*

"Ice lives the urban beat. . . . He's like the pulse of the inner city. . . . He rhymes it, he raps it, and he's got a phenomenal mind, phenomenal memory, and he's got a great body, knows how to dance to it. To me, he's like a human urban rubber band."

SBK record company vice-president Daniel Glass, on Vanilla Ice
*Rolling Stone*

"As soon as I heard, I loved them immediately . . . but I thought their hair was ridiculous."

Barbara Mandrell, on the Beatles
*The New Country Music Encyclopedia*

"Janis Joplin sings the blues as hard as any black person."

Blues musician B. B. King
*Janis Joplin: Piece of my Heart*

 ☆ ☆ ☆

"Probably the most powerful singer to emerge from the white rock movement."

*Time Magazine,* on Janis Joplin

☆ ☆ ☆

"I'm not sure that her sister really enjoys what I've done, but that was the most loyal I could be to her if she were alive today. I didn't treat her like a dead rock star. I didn't treat her like a myth to be eulogized. I treated her like knowing her as I do, as a female in the world that she was in, being in that world right now. And if she were here, I think she'd be mellowed out."

Johnette Napolitano, of Pretty And Twisted, on recording "Come Away With Me" which features unpublished Janis Joplin lyrics
*The Dallas Morning News, August 3, 1995*

87

"You've heard of the New Kids On the Block? Well, we're the old farts in the neighborhood."

Doug Sahm of the Texas Tornadoes
*The New Country Music Encyclopedia*

"Acidized country boys playing psychedelic Buddy Holly riffs."

Music historian Doug Hanners, on the Thirteenth Floor Elevators, a 1960s Austin band
*Texas Rhythm, Texas Rhyme*

"I first met him when he was appearing in Brooklyn. He had silver-rimmed glasses, gold-rimmed teeth, and looked like a hick from Texas. The next time I saw him, he wore a three-button suit, horn-rimmed glasses, had his teeth recapped, and looked like a gentleman. He was always a marvelous person . . . a sweet gentle soul."

Record producer Dick Jacobs, on Buddy Holly
*The Buddy Holly Story*

"Holly seemed to me to be an extremely sensitive individual. He looked fragile—like you could blow him over. And somehow I found myself being aware of his sensitivity, and trying to be careful of how I said things to him. Even with his country talk, he sounded like a gentleman. And he was a gentleman."

Bob Thiele, record producer, on Buddy Holly
*The Buddy Holly Story*

"He was easy to get along with, easygoing, and he was a monkey in a lot of ways, a real cutup. We sure did have a lot of fun. He was one of the best people I knew in my life."

Waylon Jennings, on Buddy Holly
*The Outlaws: Revolution in Country Music*

"Before I ever became a member of the Crickets, I was a Buddy Holly fan . . . Buddy had stage presence before he ever made it. Offstage, he was the shy next-door neighbor type, a good ol' boy. But he was totally explosive onstage."

Niki Sullivan, formerly of Buddy Holly and the Crickets
*Texas Monthly*

**90**

"Holly didn't really appeal to girls as far as a teen idol sort of thing."

Former Crickets band member Jerry Allison
*The Buddy Holly Story*

"I would go see Buddy Holly's shows and he would see mine, and back and forth there, until he made the super big time. Buddy was a very bright boy, very dedicated. He wasn't uppity, or as we'd say in the business, 'flashy.' He could tell jokes. We had a relationship that developed."

Roy Orbison
*Dark Star: The Roy Orbison Story*

☆ ☆ ☆

"It was the first major music tragedy. Heroes aren't supposed to die. And I remember thinking, 'We're not gonna hear this music again.'"

Buddy Holly fan Bill Griggs, on the plane crash that killed Buddy Holly, J. P. "Big Bopper" Richardson, and Richie Valens, 1994
*Texas Monthly*

"The only reason Buddy went on that tour was because he was broke—flat broke. He didn't want to go, but he had to make some money."

Waylon Jennings, on the ill-fated tour that ended in the plane crash that killed Holly
*Buddy Holly: A Biography*

"Holly was the first rock star to die young, pretty, and still on top."

Writer Joe Nick Patoski, 1995
*Texas Monthly*

"After Buddy died, I didn't listen to the radio for maybe ten years. I just couldn't."

Buddy's brother, Larry Holley, 1995
*Texas Monthly*

☆ ☆ ☆

"When Stevie Ray died, it was the end of Texas blues as it would be known nationally."

University of Houston sociology professor Joseph Kotarba on Stevie Ray Vaughan, 1995
*The Dallas Morning News*

91

92

"She was much better than Madonna or Gloria Estefan, the singers she was compared to, or Paula Abdul . . . . This girl could bury them. She was a very good singer."

Austin American-Statesman music critic Michael Corcoran, on Selena Quintanilla Perez, the queen of Tejano music who was murdered in 1995
*Sherman Democrat*

"This was not some sexy babe groomed by a record company. We'll never be sure of how far she could have gone."

Latin music critic/author Enrique Fernandez, on Selena, 1995
*People Weekly*

"I was the first of the singing cowboys. Maybe not the best, but that doesn't matter if you're first."

Country musician/actor Gene Autry
*You're the Reason our Kids are Ugly and Other Gems of Country Music Wisdom*

"We're hep. We're the most versatile band in America."

Bob Wills on his band The Playboys
*San Antonio Rose: The Life and Music of Bob Wills*

"Bob Wills would not allow music to be put into a straitjacket. It did not have to conform to anything but human feeling."

William Eschol Dacus, drummer, Bob Wills and the Texas Playboys
*San Antonio Rose: The Life and Music of Bob Wills*

☆ ☆ ☆

"Bob Wills put the beat into country music. He made it so you could dance to it."

Guitarist Merle Travis
*Prairie Nights to Neon Lights: The Story of Country Music in West Texas*

☆ ☆ ☆

"Bob Wills was more than his music . . . Elvis was the same. You had to see him in person to understand his magnetic pull. John the Baptist had the same pull."

Willie Nelson
*Willie: An Autobiography*

93

**94**

"Without Elvis, none of us could have made it."

Buddy Holly
*Rock Lives*

"Meeting Elvis was what really inspired Buddy to get things going."

Bob Montgomery, formerly of Buddy Holly and the Crickets, 1995
*Texas Monthly*

"I always figured I'd get to meet Elvis somewhere along the line, but unfortunately that never happened. I feel a kinship with his macho southern blues."

Barbara Mandrell
*Get to the Heart: My Story*

"Something in his voice aggravated me."

Sonny Curtis, on Elvis Presley
*Prairie Nights to Neon Lights: The Story of Country Music in West Texas*

"ZZ Top clicked from the git-go though 'cause of the nasty sound of the guitars."

Jimmy Hammond, longtime fan of the band ZZ Top
*Rock Lives*

"The Monkees were not a musical act. We had very little to do with the music business, and absolutely nothing to do with rock 'n' roll."

Michael Nesmith of the Monkees
*Off the Record: An Oral History of Popular Music*

☆ ☆ ☆

"By far the most creative group in America today."

KLIF dee jay Ken Dowe, on the musical group The Five Americans
*The Five Americans* Western Union/Sound of Love *album cover*

☆ ☆ ☆

"The public just loves a band more than they do solo artists. There's more mystique."

Don Henley
*The Dallas Morning News*

95

96

"At a get-acquainted party several days before school started, someone asked me if my real name was Bosley Scaggs and I was from Bosley, N.C. I thought it was a joke. It was pretty way out. I said yes. But the guy was serious. Somebody had told him that. Four or five days later when it came time to deny it, it seemed to stick."

William Royce "Boz" Scaggs, recalling how he got his nickname upon starting a new high school, 1980
*Sherman Democrat*

"I've always thought that Chuck Berry might have had a rock and roll heart, but he had a country soul."

Country musician Buck Owens
*You're the Reason our Kids are Ugly and Other Gems of Country Music Wisdom*

"He's so unhip, he's hip."

Record executive Dave Dorn on Pat Boone, 1996
*Sherman Democrat*

"I'm an individual that happened to love a music that by society's terms wasn't my music. But I'm definitely not a put-on or a fake. I am a country music singer. I was born with a voice to sing country music."

Charley Pride
*The Dallas Morning News*

 ☆ ☆ ☆

"I don't think I'm the best singer or the best musician in country music, but I am very proud of being so versatile."

Barbara Mandrell
*Get to the Heart: My Story*

 ☆ ☆ ☆

"I'm in love with her. She's definitely got some soul in her throat."

Stevie Ray Vaughan, on Whitney Houston
*Stevie Ray: Soul to Soul*

97

98

"It would be almost impossible to exaggerate the popularity of Jimmie Rodgers during the late twenties and early thirties when he was alive and recording. It was akin to the frenzy the big bands generated during the swing era of the late thirties and early forties. It equaled the devotion and oftimes frantic adoration of the fans of Frank Sinatra and Elvis Presley. However, there was a difference in Rodgers's popularity. It was more subtle and deeper . . . spread across all age brackets."

Texas newspaperman Townsend Miller
*Jimmie Rodgers: The Life and Times of America's Blue Yodeler*

"What Sinatra was to the forties, Presley to the fifties, and the Beatles to the sixties, Denver is to the seventies—a phenomenon."

*Newsday, December 10, 1975,* on John Denver

"There are a lot of people a lot groovier than John Denver, but few of them are worth as much."

Kinky Friedman, 1974
*The Improbable Rise of Redneck Rock*

"I'm different from Bette [Midler] or Cher or Sinatra. This might be a huge ego thing, but I tend to think of myself as the Robert DeNiro of rock. I know that's absurd, but my idols are either sports figures or Robert DeNiro."

Rock musician Meat Loaf, 1993
*Rolling Stone*

 ☆ ☆ ☆

"I am the Nureyev of rock 'n' roll."

Meat Loaf
*The Great Rock 'n' Roll Quote Book*

 ☆ ☆ ☆

"Joe is one of the great live performers. He has more charisma than Mick Jagger or Bruce Springsteen."

Country musician Jimmie Dale Gilmore, on Joe Ely
*The Dallas Morning News, September 10, 1995*

99

100

"Now I hate the word entertainer. Somebody called me once and said, 'Oh, you're such a wonderful entertainer.' I said, 'No. What I do is not for entertainment. If you derive pleasure from it, thank you.' . . . But I'm not there to entertain you."

Van Cliburn
*Van Cliburn*

"I could compare Ernest Tubb to Frank Sinatra, in that they both had distinctive styles that you wouldn't confuse with anybody else. I'd put Floyd Tillman in there with them . . . Roy Acuff had his own style, too. I think style is why a singer is either real popular or not. If you have your own style, it doesn't really matter whether you are technically a great singer."

Willie Nelson
*Willie: An Autobiography*

"Jimmie took the high road and never compromised. Unfortunately, the high road is often the long road. It took Jimmie a long time, but he's finally getting the recognition that he deserves."

Don Henley, on Jimmie Vaughan, 1994
*The Dallas Morning News*

"Jimmie had such command of his concept that he made everyone else sound slick. Jimmie was anti-slick. He was T-shirt and jeans, real working class, severely lowdown. He was anti-hippie, anti-rock 'n' roll, anti-slick. He chose NOT to do what other people were doing. . . ."

Texas guitarist Denny Freeman, on Jimmie Vaughan, 1994
*The Dallas Morning News*

101

102

"Joe is a gypsy. And he enjoys being Joe Ely. He has really pursued his artistry, but never compromised his music and tried to go mainstream with it. Even though he's never sold that many records, he's held in high esteem as an artist. When you find an artist like Joe who is a stylish singer-songwriter, you can't shape him."

MCA/Nashville Records president Tony Brown, 1995
*The Dallas Morning News*

"To be successful—in the business sense—a recording artist has to sell albums. To sell albums, a recording artist has to be played on the radio. And Ely's songs have either been too hard edged for country stations or too, well, West Texas playful for rock 'n' roll markets. Program directors like to be able to stick an artist into a convenient cubby hole, and Ely refuses to quit."

Lubbock Avalanche-Journal entertainment editor William Kerns
on Joe Ely
*Prairie Nights to Neon Lights: The Story of Country Music in West Texas*

104

LONESOME, EGOCENTRIC, SICK,
UNHAPPY, SCREWED-UP PEOPLE

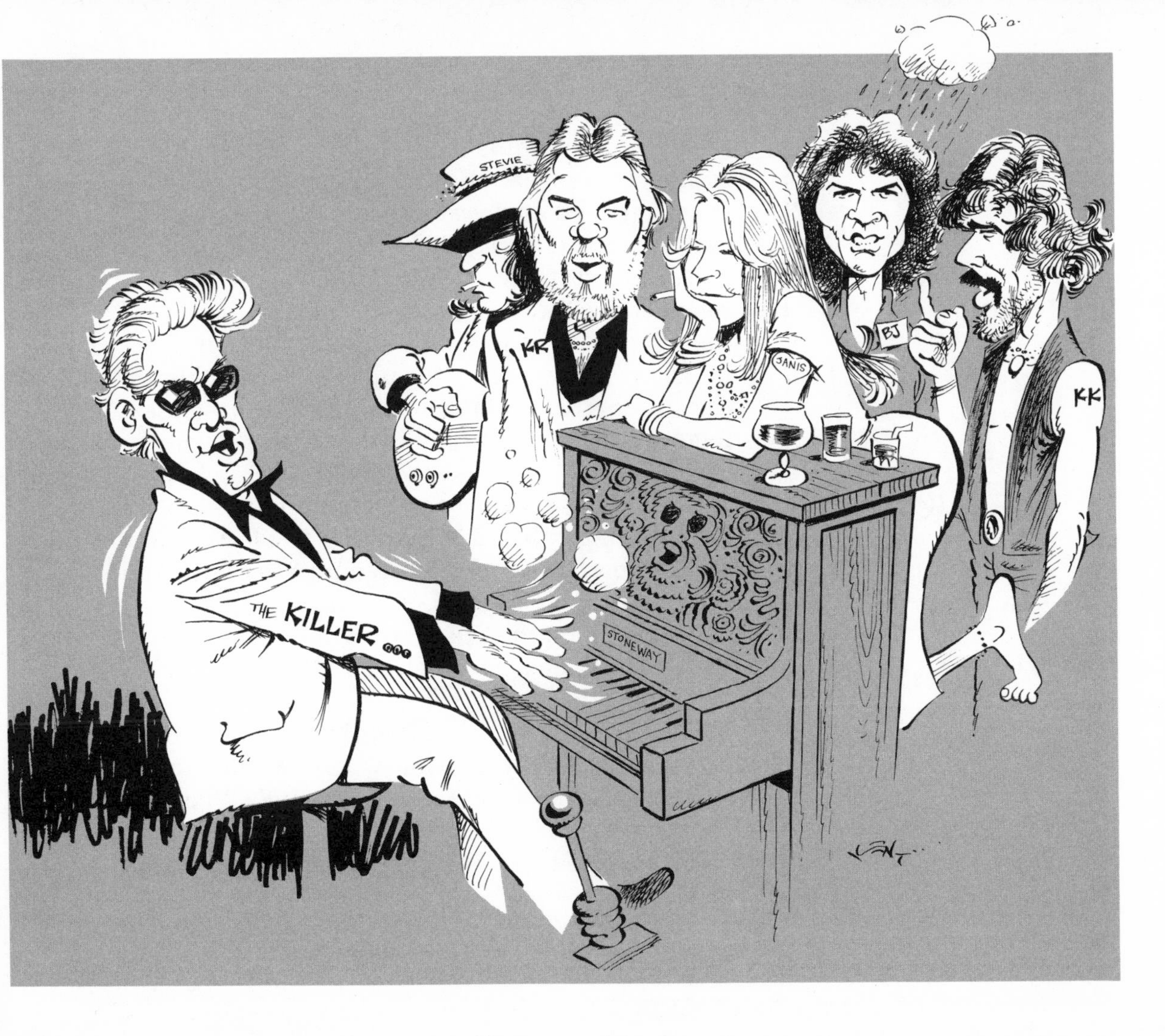
STEVIE
KR
JANIS
BJ
KK
THE KILLER
STONEWAY

106

Money, drugs, booze, limousines, groupies—they all are readily available, in abundant supply, for the superstar musician. But how much fame and fortune is enough? When does excess turn into career downfall or even tragedy? What price success?

By most standards, Steve Miller would be considered a "star" or at least "famous" for his contributions to the rock-blues-pop musical kingdom. Miller, who grew up in Dallas and learned the guitar from family friend Les Paul, has amassed fame and fortune during his thirty-year musical career.

Early blues album classics from the 1960s Steve Miller Band included "Children of the Future" and "Sailor," both of which featured boyhood friend and future star Boz Scaggs. Later, and on a more profitable note, the Steve Miller Band cranked out such number one pop singles as "The Joker," "Rock'n Me," and "Abracadabra."

That told, Steve Miller is still wary of stardom.

"I mean, there was a time when I wanted to be real famous," he told the *Record* in 1982. "Then I started watching what happens to people who are stars. They're lonesome, egocentric, sick, unhappy, screwed-up people."

"All artists go through a period where they turn on success or success turns on them. Most of them can't ride that out. I guess I was fortunate in that I had been playing and singing for thirteen years when success came. It touched me deeply, but it didn't make me crazy."

Roy Orbison
*Small Talk, Big Names—40 Years of Rock Quotes*

"Stevie was really an example of how good success can be, and how horrible it can get."

Danny Thorpe, a friend of Stevie Ray Vaughan's
*Stevie Ray: Soul to Soul*

"I believe the Lord withheld national fame from me—even during the years when I was selling millions and millions of records—because he knew I was not ready to handle it."

B. J. Thomas
*Home Where I Belong*

107

"I've been the most obnoxious superstar, arrogant . . . I'm still arrogant . . . I can be an absolute bastard . . . I've gotten all carried away with myself, being a rich man at twenty-five. Sometimes, it's difficult to deal with."

Rock musician Stephen Stills
*Small Talk, Big Names—40 Years of Rock Quotes*

"I never played any rock and roll before I went to work for Stephen. He taught me a lot, but the price was just too much for me to pay. . . . It doesn't cost money; it costs time and it costs your mind and your friends. I'd rather have my friends than any kind of financial success or critical acclaim."

Steve Fromholz, on touring with Stephen Stills
*The Improbable Rise of Redneck Rock*

"I've got a pretty strong ego myself, and Stills and I occasionally bounced off one another pretty good. We'd get drunk and holler at one another."

Steve Fromholz
*The Improbable Rise of Redneck Rock*

108

"He pretty much walks around like he's king of the world. The man has a huge ego, you know? And so do I."

Actor Dennis Quaid, on Jerry Lee Lewis on the set of *Great Balls of Fire, 1989*
*Rolling Stone*

 ☆ ☆ ☆

"She [Selena] never behaved like a superstar."

Disc jockey Jonny Ramirez, reflecting on murdered Tejano music star Selena
*Texas Monthly*

☆ ☆ ☆

"I never forgot that I was a working man's son from West Texas. When success came, I didn't go crazy and say, 'Oh, I'm above this or this.' I tried to keep my perspective."

Roy Orbison
*Dark Star: The Roy Orbison Story*

109

110

"And Buddy definitely changed a bit—he got more moody and big-headed, or whatever you want to call it."

Jerry Allison, on success affecting Buddy Holly
*The Buddy Holly Story*

"Success has never been that important to me. The minute I made $100 a week I was successful, because the most money my father ever made was $75 a week."

Musician Kenny Rogers
*Texas Monthly*

"I always wanted to be a millionaire, even when I was thirteen. I'd made up my mind to be one by the time I reached thirty."

Roy Orbison
*Only The Lonely*

"When I started out I had no thoughts of being a star. I didn't even have thoughts about making a decent living. I didn't care if I made a dollar . . . I was really more concerned with my own pleasure than whether or not they enjoyed my singing."

George Jones
*Ragged but Right: The Life and Times of George Jones*

"I find that artists in my age bracket are much more concerned with the business end—we're not just getting the money and then squandering it on fancy cars."

Country musician Holly Dunn
*The New Country Music Encyclopedia*

"If anybody in this business tells you they don't have an inflated ego, they're either lying to you or lying to themselves. You get to where you thrive on the high, that rush at night, that one hour on stage."

Kenny Rogers
*Off The Record*

111

112

"Hearing a record of mine on the air for the first time was the closest I ever came to being drunk."

Pat Boone
*Off The Record: An Oral History of Popular Music*

"Drugs can take you up, but they can also take you out. . . . I want to do music and have that express itself."

Musician Sly Stone
*Rock Lives*

"I was one of the hottest acts in the country, but I was scared to go on stage without chemicals in my body. I didn't know if I could really sing or if people really liked me or if my records would keep selling or if I would be alive next week . . . I was wasted all the time, never once performing or recording without being high."

B. J. Thomas
*Home Where I Belong*

"California isn't a real good place to get off drugs."

Waylon Jennings
*You're the Reason our Kids are Ugly and Other Gems of Country Wisdom*

"Some big changes have taken place. I haven't resolved all my problems, but I'm working on it. I can see the problems at least, and that takes a lot of pressure off. I've been running from myself too long and now I feel like I'm walking with myself."

Stevie Ray Vaughan, on success, alcohol, and drug-related problems
*Stevie Ray Vaughan: Caught In the Crossfire*

"I can't go out the same year because he's a bigger star! . . . It just decreases my chances. Two rock stars can't die in the same year."

Janis Joplin, shortly after the drug overdose of Jimi Hendrix, and shortly before her similar fate
*Buried Alive: The Biography of Janis Joplin*

113

114

"I wished I'd had something to say to Elvis Presley. When I get mad at the opportunists who are making money off his death and never once tried to help him when he was alive, I have to look at myself and admit that I didn't have anything to offer either . . . I just wish I could have done or said something, but when I was close, I wasn't any better off than he was—and was probably worse off."

B. J. Thomas
*Home Where I Belong*

"Fortune and fame aren't what they appear to be. The demands that are created by a career on that level were more than I wanted to continue at that time. I wanted to step outside it."

Boz Scaggs, on taking an eight-year hiatus from his recording career, 1988
*Rolling Stone*

"Never desire fame. Just the trappings."

Kris Kristofferson
*Talkin' Country: Down Home Philosophy and Advice from Country's Biggest Stars*

"Music or fame or money will not fill the void that only God can. I know."

B. J. Thomas, a born-again Christian
*Home Where I Belong*

"Success?  Boy, it's like jumpin' into a car doing eighty."

Country musician Clint Black
*Talkin' Country: Down Home Philosophy and Advice from Country's Biggest Stars*

"Any success you have in life belongs to not just you, but to the people who believed in you."

Mark Chesnutt
*Talkin' Country: Down Home Philosophy and Advice from Country's Biggest Stars*

116

"When I became very popular—I think they call it a household name—everybody else, without exception, would hire a publicist to get their names published, to get their picture here and there. I didn't have a PR man until I hired someone in England in 1967. So from '59 to '66 never once did I pay anyone a penny to get my name spread around. I just didn't believe, and I still don't believe, in building talent through publicity."

Roy Orbison
*Dark Star: The Roy Orbison Story*

☆ ☆ ☆

"To be in the music business you give up every constant in the world except music."

Janis Joplin
*Gone Crazy And Back Again*

☆ ☆ ☆

"There was this pressure to lay the golden egg every time, and that's an impossible feat."

Christopher Cross, 1995, on the pressure of trying to repeat the success of his Grammy-winning album of 1980
*The Dallas Morning News*

"I liken our success to Jiffy Pop popcorn. All of a sudden there's just a rise to fame. Poof."

Edie Brickell
*Rolling Stone*

"When I got tired of chasing that major label record deal, that stardom, and just said, 'I don't care anymore, I wanna do what I do the way I do it,' that's when my career really took off."

Guitarist Bugs Henderson, 1995
*Texas Monthly*

"I've got an established career. I'm not a superstar, but I do okay, and running it out of here is the best thing I've ever done."

Delbert McClinton, on moving to Nashville
*Texas Monthly*

117

"People think that people on stage are bigger than life, stronger than life. That's what makes them so special to go see. But people on stage are not superhuman—that's a myth."

Stevie Ray Vaughan
*Stevie Ray: Soul to Soul*

"I think that I may have been lucky that my relative obscurity has lasted as long as it has, because if anything does happen, and I think eventually something will happen if I stay in the business long enough, I'll be a lot more prepared than I would have been two years ago. . . . I've looked at somebody else's stardom, and seen how much it cost him."

Steve Fromholz, 1974
*The Improbable Rise of Redneck Rock*

☆ ☆ ☆

"Even once I was a singer, I never wanted to be a star. I just liked to sing because it was fun, just like people like to play tennis. It makes your body feel good."

Janis Joplin
*Janis Joplin: Piece of My Heart*

"I don't think I'm a star. I'll never be a star like Jimi Hendrix or Bob Dylan."

Janis Joplin
*Janis Joplin: Piece of My Heart*

"George Jones could have and still could do anything he wants. I've never known another singer who has the phenomenal respect as a singer by his peers as George Jones has. But I'm not sure George Jones ever wanted to be a big star. In all the conversations I ever had with him, I don't think I ever heard him tell me how big a star he was going to be someday. He just wanted to do his thing."

Buddy Killen
*Ragged but Right: The Life and Times of George Jones*

"I may be a living legend, but that sure don't help when I've got to change a flat tire."

Roy Orbison
*Only The Lonely*

120

"I never had any ambition to be a famous performer. I started out being a record producer and I never had that ambition."

T-Bone Burnett, 1988
*Rolling Stone*

"I'm the most famous obscure musician in the country."

Steve Fromholz, 1974
*The Improbable Rise of Redneck Rock*

"I suppose I'm still a cult figure. I hate that word, but a lot of good performers have been cult figures."

Delbert McClinton
*The New Country Music Encyclopedia*

"Producing album after album to critical acclaim, country rocker Joe Ely hovers perpetually on the edge of national fame."

Joe Nick Patoski
*Prairie Nights to Neon Lights: The Story of Country Music in West Texas*

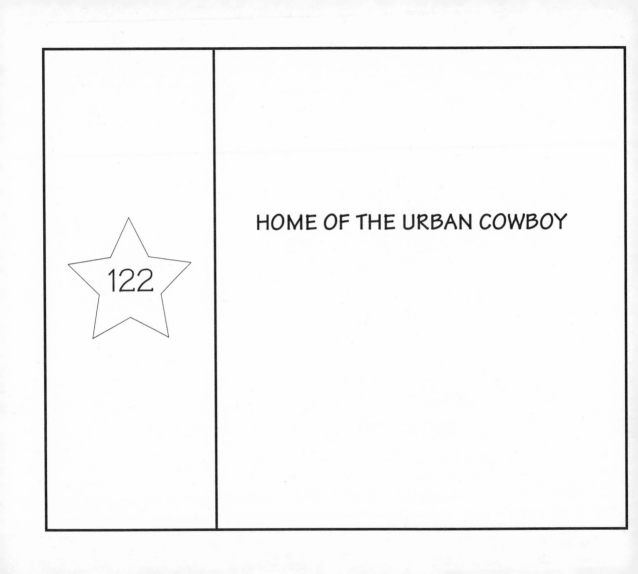

122

HOME OF THE URBAN COWBOY

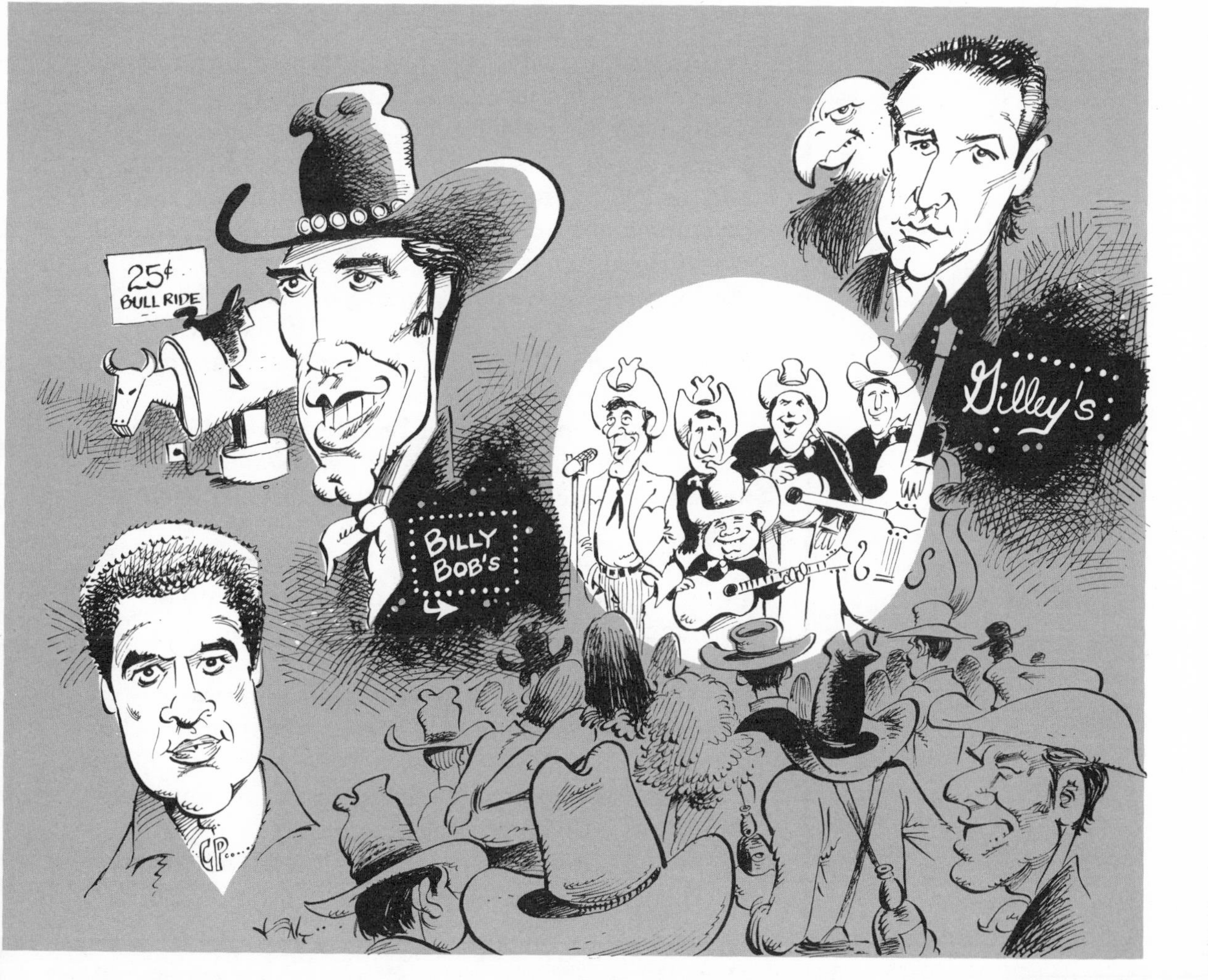
25¢
BULL RIDE
BILLY
BOB'S
Gilley's
GP

124

Many a musical career has been made or broken by live performance in a Texas venue. The state is well-known for its dives, honky-tonks, and concert arenas. Austin has long been recognized as fertile playing ground for all types of live music. By way of its many clubs, including the now-defunct Armadillo World Headquarters, the capital city gave birth to the "progressive/outlaw" country music of the early 1970s, and such stars as Jerry Jeff Walker, Willie Nelson, Waylon Jennings, and Michael Martin Murphey, to name just a few.

The long-running public broadcasting television show *Austin City Limits* continues to offer viewers an eclectic collection of musical performers each week.

In 1980, the nation watched John Travolta two-step in *Urban Cowboy*, and Gilley's Club in Pasadena, Texas, became a landmark. Billed as the world's largest honky-tonk—a title later assumed by Billy Bob's in Fort Worth—the huge and rowdy dance club offered patrons a mechanical bull on the premises.

Writer Aaron Latham offered this comment about Gilley's in a 1978 article in *Esquire:* "It's just a honky-tonk, but it looks as big as the MGM Grand Hotel or St. Patrick's Cathedral."

Alas, all good things must end. The "Urban Cowboy" fad faded, and Gilley's closed its doors in 1989.

"People down here move more slowly and drink lots of Lone Star beer and smoke a whole bunch of dope, and they play good music. They're not interested in limousines."

Steve Fromholz, comparing the Texas and Los Angeles music scenes, 1974
*The Improbable Rise of Redneck Rock*

"The main difference is that we used to drop acid and now we drop antacid."

Ray Benson of the group Asleep at the Wheel, on how the Austin music scene has changed over twenty years, 1994
*Texas Monthly*

125

126

"Austin's the only city in Texas that's worth anything. . . . [I]n Austin it seems like you can get all the different factions together and nobody seems to mind."

Folk musician B. W. Stevenson, 1974
*The Improbable Rise of Redneck Rock*

"But even when he was a big national star, the rich people here never paid any attention to him."

Buddy's mother, Mrs. Holley, on his hometown of Lubbock
*The Buddy Holly Story*

"There's nobody in Lubbock that's interested in him. I'll tell you the actual fact—if Buddy was to be alive right now with his fame and we decided to have a concert here in Lubbock, and they did not let anybody know about it but the people in Lubbock, there wouldn't be a thousand people comin' to it. It's just Lubbock, this area—they could care less. They'd rather go to a basketball game or a rodeo."

Buddy's brother, Larry Holley, 1992
*Buddy Holly: A Biography*

"We both have an appreciation of a well-written song and a story that goes along with it, painting some kind of picture about where you come from. We grew up in such different cultures and yet when you start looking into deeper things, there are a lot of similarities between New Jersey and Lubbock."

Joe Ely, on his friendship with rocker Bruce Springsteen
*The Dallas Morning News*

"Hell, I don't live in Texas. I live in Austin."

Country musician Jerry Jeff Walker
*The Improbable Rise of Redneck Rock*

"I got lost in Texas for about ten years. That's when I started gettin' into Bob Wills."

Country musician David Ball, a native of South Carolina
*Country America*

127

128

"There was a strong Austin to San Francisco axis in those days. The towns reminded me of each other. If San Francisco was the capital of the hippie world at the time, then Austin was the hippie Palm Springs."

Willie Nelson, early 1970s
*Willie: An Autobiography*

"I figured if I was going to be a songwriter, I ought to be where the songwriters are. And the best songwriters on earth are here."

Delbert McClinton, on moving to Nashville, 1994
*Texas Monthly*

☆ ☆ ☆

"I am a very proud Texan. I don't condemn those that do live in Nashville. If it weren't for Nashville I wouldn't have a career, but I see no reason to change."

Clay Walker, 1995
*The Dallas Morning News Weekend Guide*

"One of the main things I learned from Charley that has really helped my family and my career is that you don't have to live in Nashville to make it in this business. I have lived in Longview, Texas, for fifteen years. My manager is in Dallas. You don't have to move to Nashville."

Neal McCoy, on Charley Pride
*The Dallas Morning News Weekend Guide*

"I love living in Texas, it's where I'm from, and home is home. But logistically, I'd live in Nashville if my kids did not live here. But that reason alone outweighs all others."

Collin Raye, 1995
*The Dallas Morning News*

"I fell in with a bunch of great writers—Lyle Lovett, Guy Clark, Joe Ely, Jerry Jeff Walker. They inspired me to believe I could do this for a living."

Country musician Hal Ketchum, a New Yorker who found his niche in Texas
*Country Music*

129

130

"I always thought I could sing pretty good and I guess it kind of bothered me that nobody else thought so."

Willie Nelson, on leaving Nashville for Austin
*Dark Star: The Roy Orbison Story*

"I was in sort of the same situation I had been in ten years earlier. My band would fill a Texas dance hall. We were stars in Texas. But in Nashville, I was looked upon as a loser singer."

Willie Nelson, after the commercial failure of his 1971 album "Willie Nelson and Family"
*Willie: An Autobiography*

"Everybody's been saying Austin is gonna be a Texas Nashville, but I don't know. Austin's really laid back. Like if you drive from Dallas to Austin, you can feel the difference as soon as you get into town."

Steve Fromholz, 1974
*The Improbable Rise of Redneck Rock*

"Everyone in Nashville knows something is going on with country music down in Texas and it ain't in Austin. It's Beaumont."

Dan Wentworth, country music club owner in Beaumont
*Texas Monthly*

"Ever since I moved out here from Texas I've been in the Twilight Zone. I don't feel like I really belong here, and yet I can't go back to where I came from . . ."

Don Henley, on living in California
*Rock Lives*

"I'm going to become a Texas citizen. California is beyond help. This place is not."

Don Henley, 1994
*The Dallas Morning News*

131

132

"I was drafted by the state of Texas. I had to be a Texan. It was just one of those things that was meant to be."

Pennsylvania native Ray Benson
*Country America*

"Dallas was a major pit-stop on the R&B circuit. Interestingly enough, there was a general acceptance of racially-mixed audiences—at least in the black areas of town. We often went to black clubs to hear Bobby Bland or B. B. King, but no one thought it adventurous, as if we were haunting the wrong side of the tracks."

Boz Scaggs, 1977, on Dallas in the 1950s
*Creem Magazine*

"I wrote this song in the car driving from Houston to Krum, Texas, up near Denton . . . . You wouldn't believe the lack of reaction in other parts of the country when I mention that."

Lyle Lovett, introducing "Fat Babies" at a Texas concert, 1995
*The Dallas Morning News*

"You cowboys are all faggots."

Rock musician Sid Vicious, to a Texas audience on the Sex Pistols'
first tour of America
*Rock Talk*

"I'm no different offstage than I am onstage.
Because you can't come to my show without
laughing with me and laughing at me, and having
fun. And that doesn't happen at a Rolling Stones
concert."

John Denver
*John Denver*

"On stage, I make love to 25,000 different people,
then I go home alone."

Janis Joplin
*Small Talk, Big Names—40 Years of Rock Quotes*

133

134

"Offstage, he was quiet—not wild at all. But he was very uninhibited when he performed. He didn't worry about how he looked to an audience. Not that he didn't care, I don't mean that—what I mean is, he didn't hold anything back. And that was what made him so good."

Larry Welborn, a member of an earlier Holly band, on Buddy Holly
*The Buddy Holly Story*

"I really have a hard time writing songs. If I can write one a month I feel good. . . . But I do think I'm a very good performer, and that's where it's at for me."

John Denver
*Country Music*

"Any performer who hasn't the theatrical ability to put herself into lyrics for a few minutes must have something missing—like talent."

Barbara Mandrell
*You're the Reason our Kids are Ugly and Other Gems of Country Music Wisdom*

"As soon as I began singing in bars, I became hooked on crowds and the kind of energy you derive from performing and being applauded for your work. There is no rush that compares to it."

Charley Pride
*Pride: The Charley Pride Story*

☆ ☆ ☆

"You always leave the stage more pumped up than when you walk on—at least I do."

B. J. Thomas
*Home Where I Belong*

☆ ☆ ☆

"It had always been the case that my concerts were better received than my recordings. In fact, I've never been particularly happy with my singing on records."

John Denver
*Take Me Home: An Autobiography*

135

"But if you're going to have an audience out there, you can't confuse them with anything that's too weird. But if you're playing a good Texas bar, they want you to be able to play country, but you can slip in some rock 'n' roll and here and there, blues. You can pretty much play all of it through the course of the night."

Johnny Winter
*Meeting the Blues: The Rise of the Texas Sound*

☆ ☆ ☆

"When you perform, you're sitting down for friends and neighbors. You're not playing for other musicians. I have found that, generally, what works best is to pick old, familiar tunes."

Barbara Mandrell
*Country Musicians*

☆ ☆ ☆

"If it begins to look hazardous, don't do it, because performing music is also visual, I think. You try to do something, you try to create certain motions that are not distracting, that do not inflict your effort on the public. They don't need to be aware of it. They're there for some kind of enjoyment."

Van Cliburn
*Van Cliburn*

"This is where I spent the first year and a half of my career. Most of my fan club members are from Texas. I'll keep coming here until they throw me out."

Garth Brooks, on Texas, 1995
*The Dallas Morning News*

"After every tour, I swear it'll be my last. But after I'm home for a couple days, I'm ready to go back on the road."

Willie Nelson
*You're the Reason our Kids are Ugly and Other Gems of Country Music Wisdom*

"I guess you're surprised to see me comin' out here wearin' this permanent tan and singing country music, but I love country music and I just hope you enjoy it."

Charley Pride, to an audience
*Pride: The Charley Pride Story*

138

"We used to rehearse in Holly's garage because they had an old empty butane tank in there, and we'd get a great echo from it."

Sonny Curtis, on Buddy Holly
*Rolling Stone*

"We're just a garage band that gets to play in some real big garages."

Dusty Hill of ZZ Top
*ZZ Top—Recycling The Blues*

☆ ☆ ☆

"He had almost a soulmate-like connection with the Soviet audience. Somehow, Cliburn gave the people what they thirsted for. Not just musicians, but also the simple people. He opened all kinds of musical relationships to people, and it was open to nonmusicians."

Soviet pianist Lev Naumov, on Van Cliburn's extraordinary popularity in Russia
*Van Cliburn*

"We were playing underground music. Record companies didn't know what to do with us. We played every psychedelic dungeon in the country. I was on the road eleven months a year for seven years."

Steve Miller, 1983, recalling the hectic touring days of his band in the late 1960s
*The Dallas Morning News*

"You buy some dark sunglasses. Standing up front is a lot different than standing off to the side, man. Believe me, there's a big difference."

Rock musician Mason Ruffner, on moving from the role of sideman to that of leading a group, 1986
*The Dallas Morning News*

139

140

FORTY CHANNELS AND A SKY
FULL OF SATELLITES

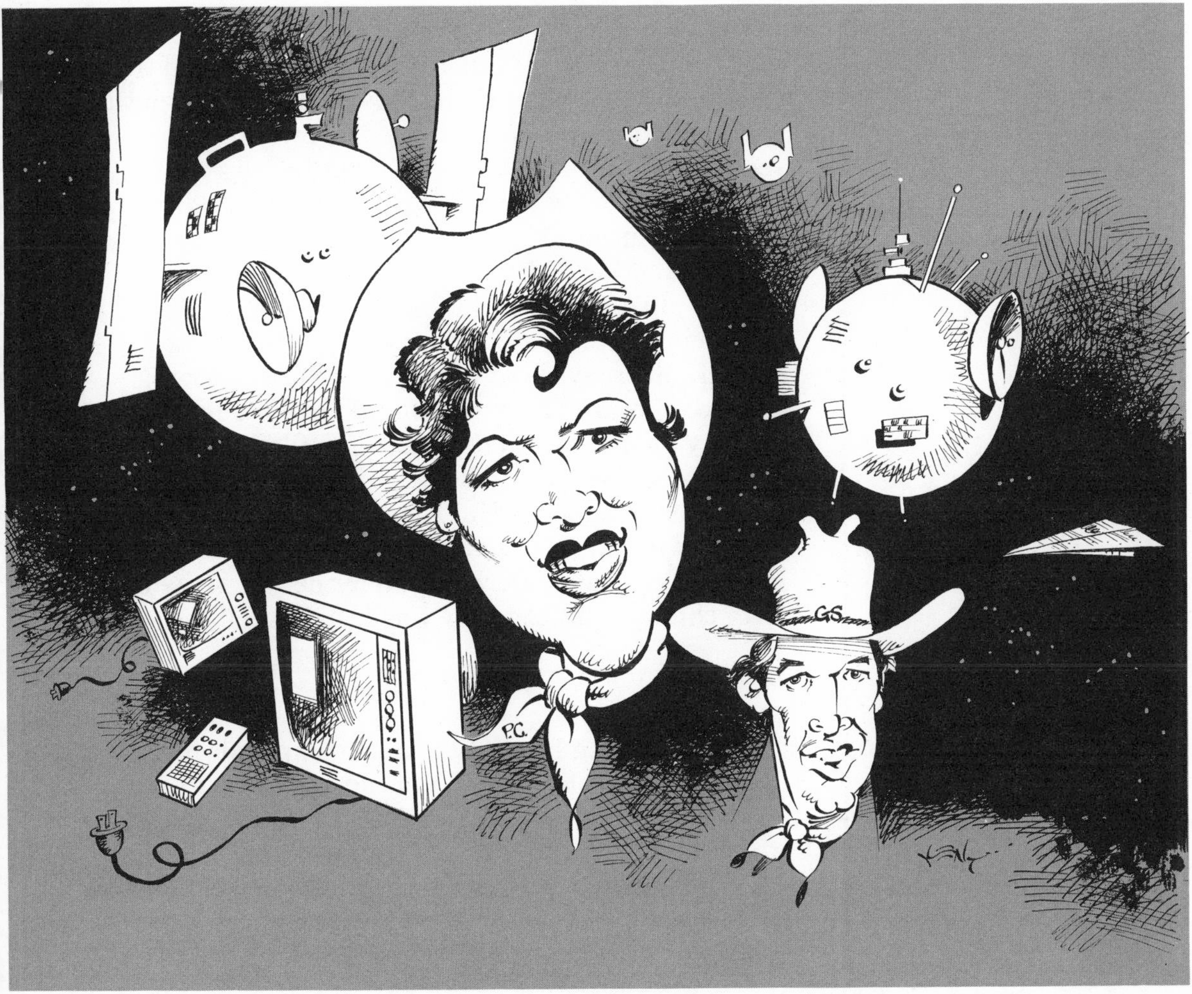
P.C.
GS

142

A number of Texas musicians have developed their own unique philosophies as they've gone through the school of hard knocks. For every "overnight sensation," there are a hundred performers who paid their dues over an extended period before finally achieving success.

Like all others, the music business finds itself in a more sophisticated world today. It seems nothing is simple in the ever-expanding world of technology. Agents, attorneys, and music videos are changing the face of music. And who would have thought that one day a vinyl record or cassette would be replaced by a compact circular disc?

As country crooner Hal Ketchum, a New Yorker who performed extensively in Austin-area clubs on his way up, said, "Life was simpler before we had forty channels and the sky was full of satellites."

"The video thing has put too much emphasis on appearance. I'll tell you, if me and Willie were starting out now, we'd be in a lot of trouble."

Waylon Jennings
*You're the Reason our Kids are Ugly and Other Gems of Country Music Wisdom*

"You try to preserve some of the things that made you who you are. And Walden Woods is one of the things that is responsible for my spiritual makeup, that is responsible for my success."

Don Henley, on his motivation for founding the Walden Woods environmental project
*American Way*

"But what really turned me around, more than anything else, was coming across a couple of good books by Albert Schweitzer. He's had a tremendous influence on my songwriting, and I'd say almost every song I've written has an underlying theme of what he was trying to get across, which was a philosophy called Reverence for Life—the idea that everything that's alive is sacred and equal."

Michael Martin Murphey
*The Improbable Rise of Redneck Rock*

143

144

"Keep your chin up and your skirt down."

Patsy Cline, giving advice to women in country music
*Talkin' Country: Down-Home Philosophy and Advice from Country's
Biggest Stars*

"The secret to life is hitting your golf ball and
watching it go out of bounds, and having enough
faith that it will hit a tree and come back in. You
can't let it bother you if you hit one ball out of
bounds."

Country musician Doug Supernaw
*Talkin' Country: Down-Home Philosophy and Advice from Country's
Biggest Stars*

"Golf and music are closely related. A large number
of musicians are golf nuts, and I believe the reason
boils down to one word—tempo. Whatever you can
think of in golf, you can relate to music. You rush
your swing, you get it out of meter."

Show promoter and golf pro Larry Trader
*Willie: An Autobiography*

"I think when you work with people who are good in anything, it kind of ups your own level. It's like that in movies, in music, and in sports. If I play golf with somebody who's really good, I'll try harder and probably have a better game."

George Strait
*Talkin' Country: Down-Home Philosophy and Advice from Country's Biggest Stars*

"If you think about failure, you probably won't even try. That's the real failure."

Tanya Tucker
*Talkin' Country: Down-Home Philosophy and Advice from Country's Biggest Stars*

"The reason you have a bad experience is to teach you not to do it again."

Willie Nelson
*Talkin' Country: Down-Home Philosophy and Advice from Country's Biggest Stars*

145

146

"Behind every dark cloud, there's usually rain."

Michael Nesmith, on the Monkees television show
*Primetime Proverbs: The Book of TV Quotes*

"I think music is a spiritual thing. I think that's why so many people who care about music and go into it have difficult lives."

T-Bone Burnett
*Written in my Soul: Rock's Great Songwriters Talk about Creating their Music*

"I never felt like I wanted to 'bop 'til you drop.' There are other things in life—and I've been doing them."

Boz Scaggs, on his extended hiatus from a recording career, 1986
*Rolling Stone*

"I think there's a kind of pianist who just will go on until they drop. And I was never certain that Van ever wanted to do that, even in the beginning. He had made his mark, he had made his money, and he was not somebody who knows nothing but music and music alone. His interests are varied, and for once in his life he wanted to pursue them."

James Mathis, a friend of Van Cliburn's, on Cliburn's nineteen-year hiatus from performing
*Van Cliburn*

 ☆ ☆ ☆

"But it seems to me that recording is taken much too seriously by most of the people who are involved in it. I guess it's the importance put on having a successful record. They say this record has to be good or your career is over. Well, I've proved that doesn't work."

Steve Fromholz
*The Improbable Rise of Redneck Rock*

147

148

"I want to make the best music I've ever made. I want it to be right and sound good whether it sells or not."

B. J. Thomas
*Home Where I Belong*

"Music is my life. I want people to feel wonderful and great when they hear my music."

Buddy Holly
*Buddy Holly: A Biography*

"I look for songs that don't sound like anything anybody else is doing. . . . But I don't want to get caught singing something that says nothing."

Collin Raye
*The Dallas Morning News*

"It's not a sin to be in the top 40."

Eagles member Don Henley on criticism that the group was too commercial, 1976
*The Story of the Eagles—The Long Run*

"The only answer to critics—and this may be the most important quality for you to develop if you desire a career as a writer of any sort—is perseverance."

Willie Nelson
*Willie: An Autobiography*

"There's no shortcut to the big time. Ain't no luck involved. It's all hard work, talent, and madness . . . You just have to do your best, and get on with it."

Collin Raye
*Talkin' Country: Down-Home Philosophy and Advice from Country's Biggest Stars*

"Trust me kid, you've got to sing. If you sing, nobody else can tell you what songs to play. If you sing, you're the boss."

Jimmie Vaughan, to brother Stevie Ray
*Stevie Ray: Soul to Soul*

149

**150**

"The main thing is to attract people. I do it. I always thought that's what a musician was supposed to do—try to draw a crowd to hear you play."

Willie Nelson
*Willie: An Autobiography*

"If people want to get stoned and tripped out on acid or Jesus, that's their business. But if things don't work out, I've got something else that will: love, appreciation, and sincerity."

John Denver
*John Denver*

"Boy, you could be the greatest guitar player that ever lived, but you won't live to see forty if you don't leave that white powder alone."

Blues legend Muddy Waters, to Stevie Ray Vaughan
*Stevie Ray: Soul to Soul*

"I made it through the Seventies alive and with my brain reasonably intact and I know that surprised a lot of people."

Don Henley
*The Story of the Eagles—The Long Run*

"I used to go to concerts completely stoned, but now I stop at four if I have a concert and start again an hour before I go on. I went into a couple of concerts smashed and when I came off, I couldn't remember them. I can trust Janis Joplin, I know she'll come off okay, but I can't trust Southern Comfort to put on a good show."

Janis Joplin
*Buried Alive: The Biography of Janis Joplin*

" . . . All my life I wanted to experiment. I experimented with drugs, I experimented with music. . . . I've always been curious to go to whatever extremes in life and get out of it."

Freddy Fender, 1995
*Sherman Democrat*

151

152

"I don't care if I'm playing before fourth graders at a gas station, right before I walk on, I think of everything that can go wrong. I used to try to calm it with a few stiff drinks. I finally learned that that [adrenalin] is a good thing. If you get rid of that, you spend the first half of the set trying to get it back."

Joe Ely, 1995
*The Dallas Morning News*

"I'm not saying I'm an angel or a saint now, because I'm not. But I've slowed down quite a bit."

Don Henley, on his wild lifestyle with the Eagles
*Rock 'n' Roll Babylon*

"There was a period of time there that I seriously considered taking up hard drinking as an occupation."

Joe Ely
*You're the Reason our Kids are Ugly and Other Gems of Country Music Wisdom*

"I just got tired of falling down. You either mature or you die."

Roger Miller, on his alcohol-related problems
*You're The Reason Our Kids Are Ugly and Other Gems of Country Music Wisdom*

"It's damned hard to sing when you're throwing up."

Jerry Jeff Walker
*The Improbable Rise of Redneck Rock*

"I think everything we go through is a test, and I don't think we're ever asked to endure anything that we can't endure."

Willie Nelson
*Talkin' Country: Down-Home Philosophy and Advice from Country's Biggest Stars*

153

154

"You have to look at bad things and figure it's just one more test of your determination. All the bad things that have happened to me have been part of a test. It's just waves. Christopher Columbus had to sail through a few of them, and look what he discovered."

Doug Supernaw
*Talkin' Country: Down-Home Philosophy and Advice from Country's Biggest Stars*

"I have a lot of energy, and I can direct it either positively or negatively. I've found out that when I direct it negatively, a lot of bad things happen—mostly to me."

Willie Nelson
*Talkin' Country: Down-Home Philosophy and Advice from Country's Biggest Stars*

"When you feel like giving up, or you're so tired you think you can't make it through the day, remember what you're working for. The reason I work so hard is so I can leave something for my children."

Tanya Tucker
*Talkin' Country: Down-Home Philosophy and Advice from Country's Biggest Stars*

"When your career is hot and the hits are coming fast, you make a lot of money in a short period of time. There are only two things you can do with money—spend or invest it. If you do either the wrong way, you're in trouble."

Charley Pride
*Pride: The Charley Pride Story*

"I've been broke before and will be again. Heartbroke? That's serious.  Lose a few bucks? That's not."

Willie Nelson, after being fined by the IRS
*Talkin' Country: Down-Home Philosophy and Advice from Country's Biggest Stars*

☆ ☆ ☆

"Falling in love isn't my big problem. Staying in love is."

Tanya Tucker
*You're the Reason our Kids are Ugly and Other Gems of Country Music Wisdom*

155

"The guitar is my first wife. She don't talk back; she talks for me. She doesn't scream at me; she screams for me—and she sho' have a sweet tune when she do."

Stevie Ray Vaughan
*Stevie Ray: Soul to Soul*

"My guitar is half my life, and my wife is the other half."

Blues guitarist Leadbelly
*The Book of Texas Wisdom*

"*Building the Perfect Beast* is more than a title for an album. It's the overriding theme of these songs. It's the way I see us going. We've got a Star Wars technology and we can genetically engineer what our kids are going to look like. But we still don't treat each other any better than we did several centuries ago. We haven't advanced in that direction at all, as individuals or as nations."

Don Henley on his 1984 solo album *Building the Perfect Beast*
*The Story of the Eagles*

156

"Some of the greatest accomplishments in the world have been performed by old men. So you're never washed up. You can always accomplish something. But you'll never do it if you retire and just sit."

Country-Western musician Tex Ritter
*Talkin' Country: Down-Home Philosophy and Advice from Country's Biggest Stars*

"My goal is [to] still be playin' Albert King's music in the year 2010!"

Stevie Ray Vaughan
*Stevie Ray: Soul to Soul*

"We lived fast and died young, so let's leave it at that."

Don Henley, on the breakup of his group, The Eagles, 1993
*The Dallas Morning News*

157

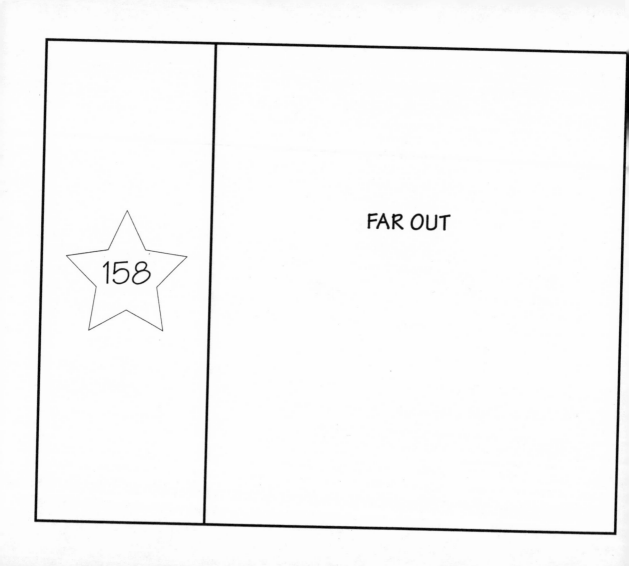

158

FAR OUT

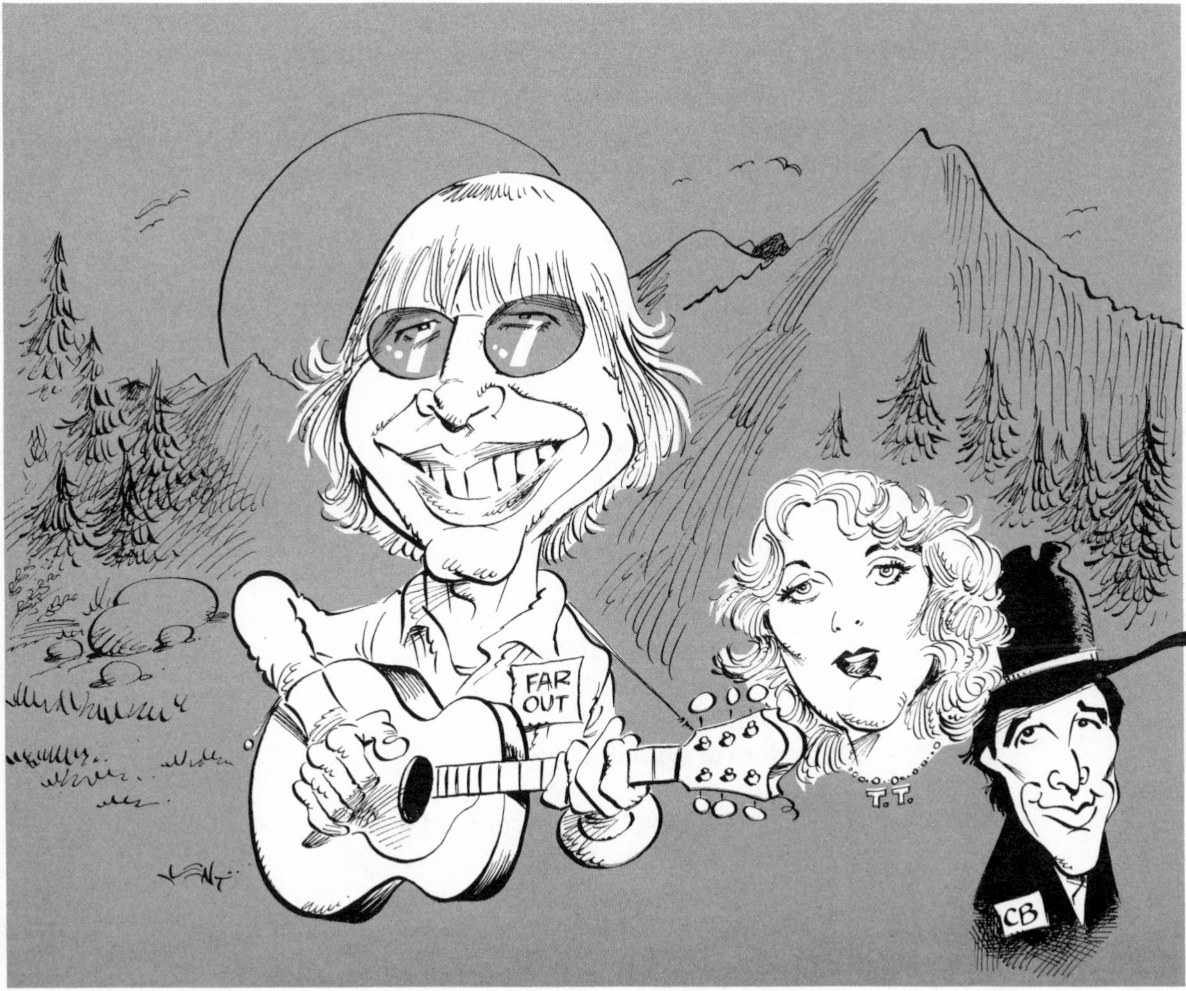
FAR OUT
T.T.
CB

160

Henry John Deutchendorf, better known as John Denver, was an Air Force brat, moving with his family from place to place. Included were stops in New Mexico, Japan, Arizona, Alabama, and Fort Worth, Texas.

After graduating from high school at Fort Worth Arlington Heights, John moved to Lubbock to study architecture at Texas Tech University. He never finished school there, opting instead to pursue a career in music.

Several years later, John Denver became a pop music superstar, zooming to the top of the charts with such classics as "Take Me Home, Country Roads," "Rocky Mountain High," "Sunshine on My Shoulders," "Annie's Song," and "Thank God I'm a Country Boy."

During the 1970s, Denver's career was aided by the national television exposure he received as a frequent guest host for Johnny Carson on *The Tonight Show*. It was also on *The Tonight Show* that Denver added a new slang expression to our vocabulary.

"The first time I appeared as guest host of *The Tonight Show,* I must have said 'far out' fifty times if I said it once," Denver wrote in his 1994 auto-biography. "Being 'cute' onstage was my way of covering up a fear I had of being seen as vacuous. Every time one of my guests would say something interesting, I would say 'far out' without even thinking; it was like having a nervous tic. In fact, for a lot of people, that's when 'far out' came into the vernacular. I have a feeling it will be in my obituary. That and the phrase 'Rocky Mountain high.'"

"The best thing about country music is that there is no dress code."

Clint Black
*Prime Time Texans,* WFAA-TV

"It's really hard to describe, but I'll give you a few things: it was macho guys working in the oil field, and football, and oil and grease and sand and being a stud and being cool. I got out of there as quick as I could, and I resented having to be there, but it was a great education. It was tough as could be, but no illusions. No mysteries in Wink."

Roy Orbison, on growing up in Wink, Texas
*Dark Star: The Roy Orbison Story*

161

162

"Texas is not quite the Wild West, but in the school systems, and in the way we grew up down here, certain things were considered important. If you were to participate in a school band or choir, you were a sissy. If you played football or basketball, track or baseball—especially football—you could be the stud of the school. Men were not pushed toward entertainment. So somebody who could perform, whether it was playing the guitar or singing, was really a rarity . . . . My dad didn't want me to play in bands. Singing and playing guitars, they're for sissies."

Guitarist Don Lampton, a high school classmate of ZZ Top's Billy Gibbons
*ZZ Top—Recycling The Blues*

"They laughed me out of class, out of town, and out of the state."

Janis Joplin, on her troubled childhood in Port Arthur, Texas
*Texas Monthly*

"I was a Future Farmer of America, yeah—F.F.A. It had another name, but we can't go into that. It was a high school course you took for credit, like wood shop. You had to have a project your senior year in order to graduate. My project was an acre and a half of cucumbers."

Don Henley
*Rock Lives*

 ☆ ☆ ☆

"At about thirteen, he was just about the height he is right now. His hands were incredible, the hands of a basketball player. He's got hands like Magic Johnson. He was also graceful and moved well. I wanted him for the basketball team."

Kilgore Junior High physical education teacher Q. L. Bradford, on the six-foot, four-inch Van Cliburn
*Van Cliburn*

☆ ☆ ☆

"He wasn't a very good dancer. He was like most musicians. He played, he didn't dance."

Helen, Roy Orbison's date at the Wink High senior prom
*Dark Star: The Roy Orbison Story*

163

"I'd always had longer hair than other boys. I was a long-haired musician before hippies came along."

Willie Nelson
*Willie: An Autobiography*

"If you wonder why you are the way you are, look at where you came from. I'm a Texas girl. That's where my roots are, and that's probably why I've always done things to excess. We like things larger than life in the Lone Star State."

Tanya Tucker
*Talkin' Country: Down-Home Philosophy and Advice from Country's Biggest Stars*

"I truly believe that Stevie wanted to be black more than anything on this earth. He was always trying to imitate that culture, the way he talked."

Mary Beth Greenwood, a friend of Stevie Ray Vaughan's
*Stevie Ray: Soul To Soul*

"Stevie's only regret was that he was not born black."

Vaughan's former manager, Chesley Millikin
*Stevie Ray Vaughan: Caught In the Crossfire*

"I don't think you should ever look up to a singer or an actor as a role model . . . because it's an image. Everything is created."

Teen R&B Singer Tevin Campbell, 1996
*The Dallas Morning News*

"They say that Virginia is the mother of Texas. We never knew who the father was, but we kinda suspected Tennessee."

Tex Ritter
*You're the Reason our Kids are Ugly and Other Gems of Country Music Wisdom*

☆ ☆ ☆

"I'm a big eater. I really like to eat, so I have to watch it. But when I go back home, to Texas, I've got to have a great big chicken fried steak, mashed potatoes and gravy, biscuits—everything! You can't always deny yourself the things you want, because that's not living."

Tanya Tucker
*Talkin' Country: Down-Home Philosophy and Advice from Country's Biggest Stars*

165

166

"Waylon is not scheduling interviews for anybody at this time. He's too often misquoted and misrepresented in print and would rather converse through his music."

Utopia Productions public relations official Bill Conrad
*The Outlaws: Revolution in Country Music*

☆ ☆ ☆

"I decided a long time ago that what I do for a living is sing, but who I am is a hunter. Because of my background in country music, with its more rural audience, I have not experienced any problems with being a hunter."

Country/opera musician Gary Morris
*The Dallas Morning News*

"These beards are part of the deal. It's another extension of the whole ball of wax; we got stuck with long beards. Gillette made us an offer to shave them off, but we had to reply that behind them, we're just too ugly."

Billy Gibbons of ZZ Top
*ZZ Top—Recycling The Blues*

"I've never met anybody in this world like me."

Vanilla Ice
*People Magazine*

"I'm going to be the Elvis Presley of the eighties."

Dallas musician Robert Lee Kolb
*D Magazine, December 1976*

"Taking care of Meat Loaf is a full-time job."

Leslie Meat Loaf, wife of rock star Meat Loaf
*Rock Wives*

167

168

# SOURCES AND FURTHER READING

Amburn, Ellis. *Dark Star: The Roy Orbison Story*. New York: Carol Publishing Group,1990.

———. *Buddy Holly: A Biography*. New York: St. Martin's Press, 1995.

Anson, Robert Sam. *Gone Crazy And Back Again*. Garden City, N.Y.: Doubleday and Company, 1981.

Bailey, Brad. "Man of Steel." *The Met*, 22-29 November 1995.

Balfour, Victoria. *Rock Wives*. New York: Beech Tree Books, 1986.

Bane, Michael. *The Outlaws: Revolution In Country Music*. A Country Music Magazine Press/Doubleday/Dolphin Book, KBO Publishers, 1978.

Bark, Ed. "Older Viewers get Politicians' Vote." *The Dallas Morning News*, 17 August 1995.

Bauder, David (Associated Press). "Posthumous Album Finally Makes Selena a National Star." *Sherman Democrat*, 6 August 1995.

Brady, James. "In Step with Larry Gatlin." *Parade Magazine,* 12 March 1995.

———. "In Step with Willie Nelson." *Parade Magazine,* 20 August 1995.

Buchholz, Brad. "Swooping in to Aid Conservation Cause." *The Dallas Morning News*, 1 July 1994.

———. "Jimmie Vaughan. Putting his own Spin on Classic Chords and Classic Cars." The *Dallas Morning News*, 7 August 1994.

Carlisle, Dolly. *Ragged But Right: The Life and Times of George Jones.* Chicago: Contemporary Books, Inc., 1984.

Carr, Joe, and Alan Munde. *Prairie Nights to Neon Lights: The Story of Country Music in West Texas.* Lubbock, Tex.: Texas Tech University Press, 1995.

Chalker, Bryan. *Country Music.* London: Chartwell Books, Inc., Phoebus Publishing, 1976.

Clayson, Alan. *Only the Lonely.* New York: St. Martin's Press, 1989.

Cohen, Jason. "The Hole Story." *Texas Monthly,* June 1996.

Corcoran, Michael. "Fans Flock to Eagles Tribute LP." *The Dallas Morning News*, 18 November 1993.

Corcoran, Michael. "The Long Run." *The Dallas Morning News*, 1 July 1994.

Cuellar, Catherine. "When Concrete, Wall Collide: Pretty and Twisted." *The Dallas Morning News*, 3 August 1995.

Dachs, David. *John Denver.* New York: Pyramid Books, 1976.

*The Dallas Morning News Weekend Guide,* 31 March 1995.

*The Dallas Morning News High Profile*, 26 March 1995.

Dalton, David. *Janis Joplin: Piece Of My Heart.* New York: Da Capo Press, 1991.

Davis, John T. "Texas—Country Music Wasn't Born There, but it Arrived as Quick as it Could." *Country America,* October 1995.

Denver, John, with Arthur Tobier. *Take Me Home: An Auto-biography.* New York: Harmony Books, 1994.

Draper, Robert. "Lyle's Style." *Texas Monthly,* October 1992.

———. "O Janis." *Texas Monthly,* October 1992.

———. "The Real Buddy Holly." *Texas Monthly,* October 1995.

Endres, Clifford. *Austin City Limits.* Austin: University of Texas Press, 1987.

169

Eremo, Judie (ed.). *Country Musicians.* New York: Grove Press, 1987.

Flanagan, Bill. *Written In My Soul: Rock's Great Songwriters Talk About Creating Their Music.* Chicago: Contemporary Books, 1986.

Freeman, Criswell (ed.). *The Book of Texas Wisdom.* Nashville: Walnut Grove Press, 1995.

Friedman, Myra. *Buried Alive: The Biography of Janis Joplin.* New York: Bantam Books, 1974.

Goad, Kimberly. "Joe Ely." *The Dallas Morning News High Profile,* 10 September 1995.

Goldrosen, John. *The Buddy Holly Story.* Bowling Green, Ky: The Bowling Green University Popular Press, 1979.

Goldstein, Patrick. "Shuffling Down to Lido with Boz Scaggs." *Creem Magazine,* November 1977.

Govenar, Alan. *Meeting the Blues: The Rise of the Texas Sound.* Dallas: Taylor Publishing Company, 1988.

Handelman, David. "Vanilla Ice." *Rolling Stone,* 10 January 1991.

Herman, Gary. *Rock 'n' Roll Babylon.* Philadelphia: Courage Books, 1982.

Hewitt, Bill, Joseph Harmes, and Bob Stewart. "Before Her Time." *People Weekly,* 17 April 1995.

Hochman, Steve. "Steve Miller: The Space Cowboy and Gangster of Love Proves there's Life after his Greatest Hits." *Rolling Stone,* 2 September 1993.

Holden, Larry, "Country's New Princess: Teen Phenom LeAnn Rimes," *Country Weekly,* 16 July 1996.

Honick, Bruce. "A Little Advice from Brenda and Tanya." *Country Weekly,* 16 July 1996.

Jinkins, Shirley. "Texas Titan George Strait is Still Country's Top Hat." *Country America,* October 1995.

Kohut, Joe, and John Kohut. *Rock Talk.* Boston and London: Faber and Faber, 1994.

Landers, Robert, and Russ Pate. *Greener Pastures: An Incredible Journey from the Farm to the Fairways.* Ft. Worth, TX: Harvest Media, Inc., 1995.

Lee, Johnny, with Randy Wyles. *Lookin' for Love.* Austin: Diamond Books, 1989.

Lee, Steven. "A Finely Tuned Business." *The Dallas Morning News,* 25 February 1996.

Leigh, Keri. *Stevie Ray: Soul to Soul.* Dallas: Taylor Publishing Company, 1993.

Mallory, Randy. "Carthage: Where Country Meets Western." *Texas Highways.* Austin: Texas Department of Transportation, June 1995.

Malloy, Merrit. *The Great Rock 'n' Roll Quote Book.* New York: St. Martin's Griffin, 1995.

Malloy, Merrit, and Emerald Rose. *You're the Reason Our Kids Are Ugly and Other Gems of Country Music Wisdom.* New York: Affinity Publishing, 1995.

Mandrell, Barbara, with George Vecsey. *Get to the Heart: My Story.* New York: Bantam Books, 1990.

Marsh, Dave and James Bernard. *The New Book Of Rock Lists.* New York: Fireside, 1994.

McKairnes, Jim. "Moving Heaven and Earth: Don Henley Fights to Save Thoreau's Walden Woods." *American Way,* 15 November 1991.

McShane, Larry. "Pat Boone Plans to Record Album for Heavy Metal Music." Associated Press, *Sherman Democrat,* 24 June 1996.

Mehle, Michael. "Steve Miller Keeps Going Back to Basics." *Sherman Democrat,* 5 October 1995.

Mingo, Jack, and John Javna. *Primetime Proverbs: The Book of TV Quotes.* New York: Harmony Books, 1989.

Minutaglio, Bill. "Texas Flood." *The Dallas Morning News,* 3 August 1995.

171

172

Nance, Scott. *ZZ Top—Recycling The Blues,* Pioneer Books, Las Vegas, 1991.

Nash, Bruce, and Allan Zullo. *Talkin' Country: Down-Home Philosophy and Advice from Country's Biggest Stars.* Kansas City, Mo.: Andrews and McMeel, 1994.

Nelson, Willie, with Bud Shrake. *Willie: An Autobiography.* New York: Simon & Schuster, 1988.

*Newsday,* 10 December 1975.

*Newsweek,* 1975.

Nicholson, Kris. "The Buzz On Boz." *Rock Spectacular.* New York: National Newsstand Publications, 1978.

Palmer, Myles. *Small Talk, Big Names—40 Years of Rock Quotes.* Edinburgh and London: Mainstream Publishing, 1993.

Patoski, Joe Nick. "Nashville City Limits." *Texas Monthly,* January 1994.

——. "Rave On." *Texas Monthly,* September 1994.

——. "The Big Twang." *Texas Monthly,* July 1994.

——. "The Queen is Dead." *Texas Monthly,* May 1995.

Patoski, Joe Nick, and Bill Crawford. *Stevie Ray Vaughan: Caught in the Crossfire.* Boston: Little, Brown and Company, 1993.

Patterson, Jim. "Tracy Byrd Gives the People Almost Everything They Want." Associated Press, *Sherman Democrat,* 4 October 1995.

Peppard, Alan. "Dad to Guv: Visit the Other Mansion More." *The Dallas Morning News,* 28 October 1995.

Porterfield, Nolan. Jimmie Rodgers: *The Life and Times of America's Blue Yodeler.* Chicago: University of Illinois Press, 1979.

Pride, Charley, with Jim Henderson. *Pride: The Charley Pride Story.* New York: William Morrow and Company, Inc., 1994.

Primeau, Marty. "Steve Miller." *The Dallas Morning News,* 27 November 1983.

Reid, Jan. *The Improbable Rise of Redneck Rock.* New York: Da
      Capo Press, 1977.

Reich, Howard. *Van Cliburn.* Nashville: Thomas Nelson Publishers,
      1993.

Richards, Tad, and Melvin Shestack. *The New Country Music
      Encyclopedia.* New York: Simon and Schuster, 1993.

Richbourg, Diane. "Ability to Bounce Back Makes Fender Legend in
      Texas Music." Associated Press, *Sherman Democrat,*
      15 November 1995.

Sasser, Ray. "Musician Morris Finds What He Seeks in Hunting."
      *The Dallas Morning News,* 10 October 1993.

Shapiro, Marc. *The Story of the Eagles—The Long Run.*
      London/NewYork/Paris, Omnibus Press, 1995.

Small, Michael and Carlton Stowers. "The Iceman Misleadath."
      *People Magazine,* 3 December 1990.

Smith, Evan. "The Comeback Kink." *Texas Monthly,* September
      1993.

Smith, Joe, edited by Mitchell Fink. *Off the Record: An Oral History
      of Popular Music.* New York: Warner Books, 1988.

Smith, Russell. "Who is Mason Ruffner?" *The Dallas Morning
      News,* 1 June 1986.

Strick, Wesley. "Boz Scaggs Treads the MOR Tightrope." *Circus
      Magazine,* 16 February 1978.

Swartz, Mimi. "Sex, Lies, and Audiotape." *Texas Monthly,* July 1993.

Tarradell, Mario. "Lone Star Long Shots." *The Dallas Morning
      News,* 25 February 1996.

———. "Raye of Hope." *The Dallas Morning News,* 19 October 1995.

Tarrant, David. "Ronnie Dawson." *The Dallas Morning News High
      Profile,* 23 June 1996.

Thomas, B. J., as told to Jerry B. Jenkins. *Home Where I Belong.*
      Waco, TX: Word Books, 1978.

Tosches, Nick. "The Devil in George Jones." *Texas Monthly,* July
      1994.

173

174

Townsend, Charles R. *San Antonio Rose: The Life and Music of Bob Wills.* Chicago: University of Illinois Press, 1976.

Tucker, Chris. "The Second Life of Ray Wylie Hubbard." *D Magazine,* March 1993.

WFAA-TV. *Prime Time Texans.* 27 June 1995.

White, Timothy. *Rock Lives.* New York: Henry Holt and Company, 1990.

Williams, Yale. "Steve Miller: Only the Strong Survive." *Record,* September 1982.

Willoughby, Larry. *Texas Rhythm, Texas Rhyme.* Austin: Texas Monthly Press, 1984.

## Acknowledgments

I would like to thank all the publications and organizations listed under Sources and Further Reading for their many contributions.

Also, a special thanks to copyeditor Jeanne Warren.

A special word of gratitude goes to my editor—Judith Keeling—and everyone else at Texas Tech University Press for their support and encouragement.

# INDEX

## A



## B



## C

## D



## E



## F



## G

Q



R



S



T

## U



## V



## W



## Y



## Z